OUR
MOTHERS'
GHOSTS

AND OTHER STORIES

Also by Marilyn Hope Lake

Buddy and the Grandcats, 2007

Susanna and the Preachers: A Dramatic Reading, 2016

Ekphrastic Writing Workbook, Volume 1, 2016

Two Cats and A Dog: Buddy and the Grandcats
2nd edition, 2016

Set in Illinois and Missouri river towns and cities from the early to late twentieth century, these plainspoken stories resurrect the past in all its glorious particulars, without sanctifying or sentimentalizing a mixed heritage of familial love and abuse. It's all here: romance, rape, domestic violence, segregation, integration, the sexual revolution, political upheaval, and each generation's backlash against the excesses of the last. *Our Mothers' Ghosts* revolves around two archetypal sisters, and Lake takes great relish in revealing the dark impulses of the golden girl Helen and the disruptive innocence of the black sheep Boots. Amid the palpable pleasures of the book's rich historical detail, there is always the shock of something blunt and honest and new.

—Trudy Lewis, author of *The Empire Rolls*

Marilyn Hope Lake's work is very impressive. Lake's tender prose transports the reader to an earlier, yet not-so-simple time that reminds us of our past and guides us to a more hopeful future. Her stories have an effect you may have seen in a classic film, beginning with an evocative black and white photograph that suddenly blooms in full, technicolor glory as the narrative springs to life.

—Daren Dean, author of *Far Beyond the Pale* and *Black Harvest*

Our Mothers' Ghosts is a wonderful collection of inter-connected short stories that gains in complexity with each story, creating a rich portrait of work and women in twentieth-century America.

—Steve Wiegenstein, Author, *Scattered Lights, Slant of Light, This Old World,* and *The Language of Trees*

OUR MOTHERS' GHOSTS

AND OTHER STORIES

MARILYN HOPE LAKE

Meadowlark
PRESS
Emporia, Kansas, USA

Meadowlark Press, LLC
meadowlarkbookstore.com
PO Box 333, Emporia, KS 66801

Our Mothers' Ghosts: and other stories
Copyright © 2023 Marilyn Hope Lake

Cover & Interior Design: TMS, Meadowlark Press

Ordering Information: Special discounts are available on quantity purchases by corporations, associations, and others. For details, contact the publisher at info@meadowlark-books.com.

FICTION / Women
FICTION / Feminist
FICTION / Short Stories (single author)
FICTION / Historical / General

ISBN: 978-1-956578-51-5 Hardcover
ISBN: 978-1-956578-49-2 Paperback
ISBN: 978-1-956578-50-8 (ebook)
Library of Congress Control Number: 2023945905

For all the strong women in my family, my "sisters by choice," and all women who strove, and strive, to overcome gender barriers and create better futures for ourselves and our families in the twenty-first century.

The past hides in the present.

—Bernard Malamud, *A New Life*

Author's Note:

In writing these stories, my use of words that may be considered offensive in today's culture is purely to stay true to the language of the times. I have no intention to offend or be hurtful. Recognizing our past helps us make a better present and future.

Marilyn Hope Lake

SHE/HER

Table of Contents

The Black Sheep
Grafton, IL — 1900-1924

"Now you take that money straight to Mr. Schlemmer at the general store and tell him I sent you to make a payment on William's birthday bike," Mrs. Hecht's stern voice matched her unsmiling face and hard eyes.

"Yes, ma'am, I will," Boots said, "But Mama, you know Mr. Schlemmer doesn't want to sell you the bike on account. What if he asks for the bike back or the rest of the money again?"

What if Mr. Schlemmer has called in Rowdy Bates from the sheriff's office to get the bike back? Boots thought. She got almost as much pleasure out of thinking this as saying it out loud to her mother would have been. She was generally fed up with William's habit of stealing whatever he wanted, and their mother paying for these "presents" to protect him. Visions of her younger brother William being led away to the county jail, his curly-haired head bent, his eyes cast down, hands cuffed, and ankles shackled, wearing a dingy blue and white-striped uniform with PRISONER emblazoned across the back, cheered her to the point of a smile.

"Don't you bother to be thinking about anything else but the task at hand." Her mother's voice intruded on her pleasure. "If all my children were as difficult as you, Laura Mae Hecht, I'd be in the state hospital at Alton, sure as you know. You do aggravate me!"

Boots was out of hearing range before her mother's speech was finished, but she knew it by heart, and it troubled her more than she realized. She had never been able to please her mother, no matter how hard she tried. Everything she did, from what she wore to the way she combed her hair, and most especially anything that she considered fun, solicited the same criticism from her mother. "You're our black sheep, Laura Mae. Every family has one."

The people of Grafton, to a soul, each had an opinion on practically anything to do with the Hechts — Laura Mae and Helen, their older brother Daniel, the youngest child William, Mr. Hecht, who was top man at the gun powder mill, and his wife, known as "Old Mrs. Hecht," even though she was a full five years younger than he. Laura Mae was a tomboy and everyone except her mother called her Boots. Her father gave her the nickname when she was a toddler after he found her trying to walk in his hunting boots.

At fifteen, she was a lanky, flat-chested girl, unlike her twelve-year old sister, Helen, whose bosoms were already a burden on her small frame. They were both blondes in the tradition of their German and Scandinavian heritage, but Helen's hair was lighter, some Graftonians said "Like wheat shining in the sun." Others thought Laura Mae's darker hair looked "richer, like clover honey." The two sisters' lives were played out as openly as the three-hundred-year-old turtles' that inhabited the giant aquariums at Finn Inn, a restaurant where customers ate a deep-fried catfish or crisp, accordion-shaped buffalo sandwiches and watched their meal's cousins swim by through the glass at the end of the heavy wooden booth.

The Hecht family home was situated in the most well to do part of town, high up from the river on the east side. To get to Schlemmer's, Boots took the long way, down and under the bluffs.

"Hey, Boots Oakley, where's your gun?" A boy yelled at her from up the hill.

"Come on, Boots, it's Saturday. Let's go shoot some birds," another boy yelled. The Hayes brothers' bright red hunting shirts stood out against the white limestone bluffs they were climbing. Then she saw a third boy, her brother William.

An ever-present anger rose to the surface at the Hayes brothers' taunting use of her father's pet name for her. Worse, William was with them. Good thing her mother could not see these bluffs from the house.

Boots excelled at anything athletic. She played boys games and sports all her life. Although she hung out with the Hayes brothers, too, the only boy she had any admiration for was Phil Anderson.

Phil was seventeen, almost a man like her father and Daniel. He was the one boy in town that Boots liked unequivocally. She found some fault in all the others. She was first attracted to Phil's gentle strength and interest in music. He played the violin like his immigrant father before him. Even after she knew him better, no flaw surfaced to push her away. Lots of boys had crushes on her, including both of the Hayes brothers and the minister's son. What she liked the most about Phil was that he treated her like a friend and a girl, too.

Look at them, she thought, *carrying their rifles up on those rocks. If I was there, we would walk around the backside where we'd be less likely to slip, but it takes a brain to think of that. Nothing but showoffs! How does William get away with things all the time?*

Go on William, step on a loose stone. Just as she thought this, she imagined she saw her younger brother slip a little, stumble forward, almost lose his balance, as his rifle clattered down the side of the bluff.

"Come on, Boots Oakley," her brother yelled. The vision passed.

There should have been four of them, climbing like mountain goats, waving and calling at other friends below. But every Saturday for the last month, Boots had been forced to go to Mr. Schlemmer's with a payment on the red sidewalk bike her younger brother was getting for his ninth birthday, November 5th, now just two weeks off. Every Saturday morning she endured the humiliation.

"I don't care if your mother does think you Hechts are royalty here in Grafton. In my store you pay for bikes before you take them home." Mr. Schlemmer looked at her as if she had taken the bike. He might as well, she thought. Her mother would never send William down to face the store owner; and, as everyone knew, Mrs. Hecht never left her house and fenced in yard except to go to the hotel in Brussels for an occasional Saturday night dinner.

"Credit is for necessities. Why I ought to tell your father."

"Yes, sir." *You won't tell my father you old blowfish. You're too afraid of mother, of what she might do to stop the flow of powder mill money through your cash register. You faker, yelling at me.* Boots suddenly felt a sense of pride at her mother's strength of will.

"Tell your mother that if that boy of hers takes one more item!"

"You'll what?" Her eyes, full of pride and challenge, fixed on his.

"Just tell her." Mr. Schlemmer said, beaten.

"Yes, sir." Boots said, leaving quickly before she acted her anger out further. *William's a plague,* she thought.

She would have liked to be there when it actually happened, to have seen it. William walking up to the new Schwinn bike which sat outside for sale display, marked down all of three dollars, putting his books in the bag behind the seat, throwing his leg over the bar, not caring a bit whether he got chain oil on his good school trousers, and riding home to the yells and cheers of all his schoolmates while Mr. Schlemmer hit the clanging store bell with the stick end of a broom to call for help. Second only to the toboggan he took last Christmas, when he was just eight years old, the bike was the biggest gift William had ever "picked out for himself." That's how their mother phrased it.

Boots was smiling, but her chest hurt. The inside felt tight, like skin stretched over a drumhead. Maybe she would go shooting with the boys after she finished her household chores. Her nickname wasn't Boots Oakley for being a bad shot. Kill a crow or two, or maybe chance on a turkey. It wasn't turkey season, but she knew that even her stern mother would not turn her away with a turkey over her shoulder.

Her older brother Daniel and her father would be disappointed in her though. When they taught her to shoot, they impressed on her how important the game laws were.

"They're for the protection of the game and the hunter," her father had said.

"The laws control the hunters, the hunting controls overpopulation," Daniel added. Boots had seen the exact same words in an old issue of Daniel's National Rifle Association magazine.

Her father completed the lesson. "You know, everything works better when everyone works within the rules. Hechts always play by the rules."

Walking home from making a payment on William's "birthday present," Boots thought that living in their family was like living at exactly opposite ends of the world at the same time.

She thought of the last time she watched from under the hall stairs outside the opened pocket doors to the dining room while her mother and father had dinner alone.

• • •

Her father sat at one end of their long dining room table, tired and impatient, anxious to get to the card game, homemade liquor, and company just one house down the hill at his friend Tom O'Brien's. Her mother sat at the other end, starched and prim, even after a long day of scrubbing and shining. Her father was tapping his fork lightly against the edge of the china plate, a nervous habit Mrs. Hecht always upbraided him for, but not that night.

"Dinner's over, Minnie," Nate Hecht said. "We haven't spoiled it. Now you can tell me how William came to get this present early."

Her mother nodded a silent acquiescence. The china tapping seemed louder for her silence.

"Helen told me he's ridden it so much that it hardly looks new anymore," Mr. Hecht continued.

"I saw no harm in letting the boy have the bike early. His birthday is so close to first snow," Mrs. Hecht said. "This way he'll get plenty of use out of it before he has to put it up for the winter."

"I'm against it, the boy needs to be taught patience." Mr. Hecht was quiet a moment, watching his wife. "But I never feel it's worthwhile to go back and try to undo something that's done."

The tapping stopped, and Boots knew her mother had won. He pushed away from the table, folding his napkin up under the china plate. This was the sign of Daniel Hecht Sr.'s imminent flight.

Boots remembered the way her mother patted the slightly yellowing blonde bun at the back of her head, folded her napkin under her china plate, and rose to stand unmoving at her place until her husband turned to walk out toward the hallway to get his evening coat and hat. Following him to the door, she helped him on with his coat, handed him his hat, and asked him if she should stay up.

"No, you need your rest, and I'll probably be late."

Boots recognized a quick expression of relief on her mother's face as the memory faded.

• • •

By Saturday afternoon, Boots and Helen finished all their chores and were on the way to the outdoor roller-skating rink on the square. This was the one thing the sisters always agreed on. They both loved to skate. William had gone on ahead with the Hayes brothers. All three boys made it off the bluffs without a scratch.

It had been two weeks since the sisters were allowed to go skating because the last time they went, one of the girls at the rink decided to invite everyone home for a dance party instead. Although this particular girl was not on Mrs. Hecht's approved list for her daughters, Boots heard that Phil Anderson was going after he got off work; and she went anyway. Helen promised to keep quiet, but when pressed about why she was home earlier than her sister, she told.

The next week neither sister got to go skating. Mrs. Hecht made Boots stay home because she went to the party, and Mr.

Hecht made Helen stay home because she tattled. For once this had not caused a fight between the sisters because Helen, whose interest in boys had blossomed as soon as her bosoms, understood her sister's desire to see Phil Anderson more than Boots did.

With a few exceptions, the sisters got along much better as teenagers than they ever had. Boots was always a tomboy, and Helen was the little princess, at least until William arrived. No matter what punishment she received, Boots could not resist the vision of Helen crying over untied ribbons and loosened shoestrings or mud on her dress.

. . .

Mrs. Hecht had never had much time for Boots, even when she was the youngest child. Boots was born one year after the death of Leonard, a six-week-old baby boy, from whooping cough. When she was pregnant again, Minnie Hecht dreamed of having another little boy to take Leonard's place. She got a girl instead.

She took fastidious care of the child, but the truth was that she simply did not want a girl. Mr. Hecht and Daniel gave the baby the love her mother denied her. Boots never lacked for love. It was mothering she missed. Three years later, Helen was born, and she was given all the attention and mothering Boots wanted. After William was born, the wizened six-year-old Boots began to feel a bit sorry for Helen because now that there was a prince in the house the little princess got much less attention.

The day William was introduced to the family was warm for November, almost seventy-five degrees Fahrenheit, Indian summer. The two little blond girls stood quietly on the porch, painstakingly dressed in matching outfits as if they were twins. They wore long-sleeved cotton twill dresses with the same pattern. Each dress had a thick velveteen belt with a big velveteen buckle. Boots's was navy blue and Helen's was red. They wore long white stockings so that no skin was bare below their dress hems, and they had matching high-topped black dress shoes. They peered out from under the turned down brims of dome-shaped hats, with velveteen bands that matched their belts. A nosegay of fall flowers was attached to each hat band.

They stood together. Boots at six was a full five inches taller than Helen at three. The sisters watched and listened for any sight or sound of their parents' new touring car. Mr. Hecht had left three hours earlier, promising to return with their mother and a surprise.

Helen turned her soft blue eyes, full of happy anticipation, from the cobblestone street and looked at Boots, who stood stiff and still as the wooden Indian outside Lemer's tobacconists. "Why isn't Mummy here, yet?" Helen asked. "I'm tired of waiting."

The girls had been standing on the porch since mid-morning when the woman their father hired as a temporary cook, housekeeper, and nanny dressed them and told them to go out front and wait.

"I want Mummy to be home right now!" Helen stamped her black leather crossband shoe and shook her head for emphasis, throwing her domed hat off balance.

Boots continued to stare over the picket fence and down the long street, which was quiet because all the other children in the neighborhood had gone to school hours earlier. The six-year-old was transfixed, watching the street, listening for sounds, even trying to sniff the air, the way Sheba their cat did when she sensed that something was about to happen.

"I want my Mummy!" Helen started walking around in a circle stamping her feet, bouncing her hat with every stamp.

Then, as if Helen's war dance had succeeded, both girls heard the sound of the family's touring car coming up the cobblestones. As the car drew closer, they saw their mother sitting straight-backed and stiff-necked beside their father, with a large laundry basket in her lap. She wore a deep purple velvet cloak and a matching purple hat with a dark green satin tie in a bow to the right of her chin, making her look oddly regal and out of place at the same time.

Neither girl moved, though both wanted to run down the front path and grab their mother's skirts as soon as their father helped her out of the car. Daniel, who also heard the new Packard Six approach, came out onto the porch and stood behind his little sisters. He had inherited both his parents' Nordic looks, and he towered over the younger children.

Mr. Hecht opened the car door for their mother, lifting the big basket from her lap, then holding out his hand to help her out of the car. Mrs. Hecht took the big step down, gingerly at first, but with one thick-heeled ankle-high shoe on the ground, her second step down was firm and self-assured. She was home, safe from prying eyes and general interference with her family life. She would soon be well enough to assume her role as head of the household again.

Minnie Hecht barely noticed her two daughters waiting to hug her skirts as she brushed past them and stepped to the side. "Daniel, get the door for your father," she said.

After their father passed with the basket, Mrs. Hecht crossed the threshold into the foyer, half-turned towards the sisters, and without looking at either one, said, "Well, come on girls. Come in and meet your baby brother, William."

• • •

At the skating rink, Boots was first out on the floor. Round and round she skated until all thoughts of Mr. Schlemmer, and her mother and William, and the problem of boys in general, were out of her head, replaced by the sheer joy of skating well.

"What you daydreaming about, Boots? Me?"

The startled girl lost a beat as she looked up to see Phillip Anderson smiling down at her. Phil was a full foot taller than she was. He had great dark eyes that overwhelmed the rest of his rather thin and scholarly face. Today he had a patch stuck under his nose on the upper lip. He had been wearing it since Thursday. Helen said it made him look like Ichabod Crane, but Boots barely noticed it. He skated up beside her and was close enough to put his arm around her if he wanted to, which was exactly what she had been thinking of.

"Don't kid yourself," she snapped back. "I don't think about you all that much."

Since the beginning of summer, Phil had been courting Boots, and she had responded to him as a very good friend. By now she was having confusing, sometimes romantic, sometimes physical feelings about him. In school, if he crossed her mind, she would lose track of where they were in their lessons. When reminded to pay attention, she would blush, something she had never done before, perhaps because Helen blushed with abandon.

When she undressed at night, if she had seen him, or had been thinking about him most of the day, she would find a light smear of sticky white fluid on her panties. If he stood close to her, every sense became heightened, causing her to recognize his scent and feel his presence like a change in the thickness of the air on a humid day. Once when he walked up behind her and put his hand on her shoulder without warning, his unexpected touch radiated through her from her shoulder to her toes. Today she was surprised to see him because he usually worked on his father's ferry boat all day on Saturdays.

Phil sensed that she was having feelings for him that she had never experienced before and teased her lovingly. "Come on, be honest. Weren't you thinking just one little thought of me?" he said. "Maybe, just one."

They were skating hand in hand now. She felt stronger held in his firm grip, yet somehow threatened by the graceful sway of his lean body next to hers. He turned backwards and was swinging her around as they skated.

"Night and day, my Laura. I think about you night and day."

Along with a heady rush of pride at being able to keep her balance, there was a sweet tightness starting deep inside her body, rising through her, causing her to shiver ever so slightly. Three months ago, she would have laughed him off the floor for talking this way.

The song ended and Phil pulled her around into his arms, holding her briefly, before they toed to a stop. Helen skated up to where they were standing, her face flushed and smiling, her red skating skirt swirling as she turned.

William pulled in behind her, chirping, "Boots has a boy-friend! Boots has a boyfriend!" his head shaking back and forth in time to the chirping.

"Come on, brat. Skate with your sister." Helen said, pulling William by the hand and onto the skating rink floor again. Helen's instincts were honed when it came to boy/girl situations.

"Let's go out again." Boots led the way. "Last dance. They'll play something romantic."

"Won't Helen tell your mom?"

"Maybe, but I don't think so," Boots said. *She knows I saw her kissing Johnny Mayes behind the fire bush hedge after school Friday,* Boots thought. *I don't think so at all.*

They skated with their hands crossed under the latticed ceiling with the sun shining brightly through the small squares. Boots was radiant. She had never felt so content.

Suddenly, Phil motioned to stop. His face was paper white. Before they could get off the rink floor, Phil stumbled and fell to one knee. As she was helping him up, her arm brushed his forehead. It felt like the bottom of a hot iron. Then she noticed that the patch had come undone on one side and the angry red knot on Phil's lip looked larger.

She tried not to panic. She had seen fever before, but not as bad as this since the night her mother dunked William in a tub of cold water. They headed to the benches at the side of the rink.

"Are you all right?" His color was coming back.

"I'm just dizzy. It must be the medicine Doc Stokowski gave me."

"That quack," Boots said. "What for? When?"

"It's nothing. I was trying to pop this pimple on my lip; and instead of coming to a head, it got bigger."

"So?"

"So, Mom was worried. Crazy. Something about infection going to your brain. She made me go see Doc Stokowski." Phil was acting normal again, but his eyes had a glazed look, and his forehead was still iron hot.

"You should go to Alton to St. Joseph's emergency room. That old coot isn't good for anything but colds and delivering babies."

"It's just a pimple, Boots. A giant, prize winning, blue ribbon at the state fair pimple. Doc gave me some poultices and some sulfa pills. I'm supposed to rest, not exert myself. That's why I'm not working the ferry today."

"You sure do listen good, don't you!" Boots said. She wanted to hit him and hug him at the same time; she felt tears coming to her eyes. "What are you doing here if you're not supposed to exert yourself?"

"Being with you is never an exertion. It's easier than breathing."

Boots knew this was supposed to make her feel good, that lovers said such foolish things to each other and were perfectly serious. She just thought it sounded shallow, not true. Phil was her best friend, and she expected better from him than throw away lines you might hear in a song. Still, there was something different in the way he was looking at her, as if to see her totally.

"I knew you'd be here. I wanted to see you, here, where we could be almost alone," he said. "Don't be angry, be my girl."

He had regained more of his color. Skates off, they stood and walked over to the door to wait for Helen and William who were just now getting off the rink.

Phil turned to her, as serious as she had ever seen him. "Boots, do you understand how much I want to be with you, alone?" he said.

Mama would never allow that, she thought. Her mother actually liked Phil Anderson. His younger sister Julie was in Helen's group of friends. Mrs. Hecht had allowed Phil to come to dinner one Sunday night with Julie.

Phil also had been allowed into the fenced in yard to play croquet with them. Another rainy Sunday afternoon, Mrs. Hecht played the piano and Phil joined in with his violin, while Julie, Helen, William, and Boots leaned against the old grand piano in wide-eyed amazement at the sight of Mrs. Hecht having a good time. When Phil and Julie left, Mrs. Hecht looked at her children and exclaimed. "Now there are two genuinely well brought up young people. You could all learn from them!"

Just like you, Mama, Boots had thought. *Always looking at the surface. If you could hear the things Helen and Julie talk about, and see them with boys, you wouldn't let Julie any-where near this house. You don't know Phil at all. He is nice, but he might be a jerk for all you know.*

• • •

"Meet me at the abandoned quarry up by Blue Pool tomor-row morning." Phil's voice was so deep it sounded as if it were coming from the depths of a hundred foot well.

"I can't," Boots said.

"Please. Please, Laura Mae."

"I'm supposed to go to Sunday school and church with Helen," Boots said, thinking he made it sound so beautiful when he said her full name. "William is spending the night with the Hayes boys, and mother wants me to walk with Hel-en."

"Will Helen tattle if you skip it?"

"Who knows."

"I'll bring something for a picnic and a canvas tarp to sit on. They're coming now. Tell me you will." He was pleading.

"I'll try," Boots said. *Is this really going to happen?*

I'll wait for you at the crevice on the south side of the quarry? Can you find it?"

"Sure, I went hunting there with my father once."

"Promise me you'll come."

Youthful desire shone in Phil's eyes. Boots did not under-stand this look, but it moved her. She smiled at him. "If I can get away with it, I'll be there. When you hear the church bells chime for Sunday school, I'll be on my way."

William left with the Hayes brothers, and Phil walked Boots and Helen to within a block of their house. He looked better, but Boots noticed that he was walking slower than usual. They both turned at exactly the same moment for a last look. He waved and she waved back. She stood there a minute longer, and he turned around again, waiting for her to go.

Helen finally pulled her away. "We don't want to be late now, do we? Not if you want to see Phil ever again in your lifetime."

Boots knew she was right. Her mother would be furious if they were late because of a boy, even Phil.

After they had their "children's supper" in the kitchen, it was already dark. Boots and Helen helped with the dishes, and then Helen went upstairs to listen to the Victrola. Boots could hear her playing the songs they skated to that afternoon.

Once Mrs. Hecht started getting the dining room ready for a late dinner with her husband, Boots was out of her mother's thoughts for the evening. It was easy for Boots to get out again. She said she was going to check on William's rabbits, make sure that he fed them before he left. It was just as easy for Boots to sneak her rifle and a change of clothes in a canvas bag outside with her.

The rifle was a stroke of genius, she thought. *If I get caught, I'll tell Mama that we were hunting.* The laundry bag served two purposes—holding her breeches, the rust-colored doe skin shirt Phil liked, and her climbing boots, as well as a place to put her Sunday dress and patent leather shoes when she changed. Boots hid it all in the ditch along the road behind the schoolyard. She put shells for her .22 in the laundry bag and laid it under the rifle case to prevent the rifle from getting dirty or wet. There was no water in the ditch though. October had been dry as a bone. She covered it all with autumn leaves that had fallen from the big Norway maple that filled that corner of the lot. In the morning, on the way to Sunday school, she would fake stomach cramps. Even Helen would never mention Boots missing church because of her time of the month. No one talked about such things.

Boots lay awake wrapped in her eider down, watching the moon, thinking about being alone with Phil. She put her hands up under her flannel pajamas, then brought them slowly back down over her breasts, then down her side to below her hips. There was a perceptible curve at her breast, slight but there, like the curve of a rifle stock. Her nipples were taut and hard, rough to the touch like the edges of rock flakes chipped off the bluff.

She could not stop thinking about tomorrow. Would he kiss her? He had kissed her before, once on a hayride, and once out behind the hedgerow at a picnic. She wondered if Phil would want to touch her breasts or touch her below when they were alone. She knew what couples did up at the quarry, but that was in the summertime.

It was almost November, and though they were enjoying a crisp, bright Indian summer, it was cold. Surely it was too cold. The tightness and tingling sensation she felt when she and Phil were skating was back and had become unbearable. She wanted to rub herself free of it, but something about that felt more wrong than usual.

She knew that tomorrow was going to change her whole life. She felt excited and afraid at the same time. She finally fell asleep, warm and safe under her eider down, in her white canopy bed.

Her mother was shaking her out of the deep sleep that had finally overtaken her. "Mrs. Anderson just called to say Phil won't be meeting you this morning."

"What?" Boots wasn't faking. Not awake yet, she had forgotten about going to the quarry.

"A picnic? At the quarry Mrs. Anderson said. You and Phil." Her mother's voice rose on the word quarry.

Boots knew that Phil would never have told his mother about the picnic. Helen must have seen her sneak the gun and clothes out. But how would she know about the picnic?

"Oh, Laura Mae, you are my black sheep all right. Planning to sneak off up to the quarry with a boy three years older than you. I have half a mind to blister you, but . . ." Her mother's eyes looked upset, worried.

"What? What's happened? How do you know about the picnic?"

Boots jumped out of bed and was pulling her breeches on over her pajamas. "Where's Phil? Something's happened to Phil, hasn't it?"

"Phil is very sick," her mother's voice was unusually kind. "The boil on his lip has grown. The whole side of his face and forehead are swollen, and they're afraid the infection has reached his brain."

"That can't be. I saw him yesterday. He was all right yesterday!"

"Was he? Helen said he didn't seem right to her."

"We're going on a picnic. You're just trying to stop us."

"Dr. Stokowski is there. He's going to try to lance the boil."

"I'm going to him."

"You can't. You have your morning chores, and you have to go with Helen to church."

All the anger of the past month, of the years, spilled out. "You do the chores, Mother! You take Helen to church or get William home to walk with her. Better yet, let her go by herself!"

Mrs. Hecht stood silent as the girl screamed out her anger.

"William and Helen can do no wrong. William and Helen never have to do anything but keep their rooms straight. But me, I do everything for you. And you never even notice. You never say I did a good job, you just give me more and more to do."

Mrs. Hecht turned and began making the bed without speaking. When she did speak, her face was turned away from Boots, and her voice was matter of fact.

"William is spoiled. There's nothing I can do to change that now." Mrs. Hecht was plumping up the pillows. "And Helen doesn't worry me like you do. I understand her. I can read her thoughts. You were always a puzzle to me. Where is your pink coverlet?"

"I don't know, on the closet floor probably."

"Get it," Mrs. Hecht said. "I keep you busy to keep you out of harm's way."

"Harm's way?" Boots had not moved an inch.

Her mother turned and faced her, shaking her finger at Boots, shaking all over. "You think you can play with boys all your life, and they'll never hurt you. You don't know men like I do. Men like my first husband. Men like your father."

"What?" Boots was shocked, her mother never talked about anything personal.

"I was always afraid that someday they would gang up on you. It's happened before."

"Not, Phil. He would never hurt me."

"Any man will hurt you."

"What do you know about men? Or anyone? You're never around other people. You never leave this house." Boots started toward the door. "I want to go see him. You have to let me go."

"What could you possibly do, child?" Her mother, calmer now, was just standing there.

"I could be there with him. He would want me with him." There was a certainty in her voice, a new understanding.

"He wouldn't know you." Mrs. Hecht strained to keep her voice calm and firm. "His mother said he's been delirious since early morning. Just came out of it once, for a few minutes; that's when he told her you were waiting for him at the old quarry. That's why she called.

Boots's mother walked closer to her now. The girl thought she was going to take her into her arms, but she put her hands on her daughter's shoulders instead and looked at her with the old rigidity.

"You are going to do your chores and go to church with Helen." Her grip tightened. "Go to church and pray for the boy. Maybe God will spare him. In any case, God's spared you from bringing shame on this family."

At that moment, Boots hated her mother and was sure she always would.

• • •

Phil Anderson died Sunday morning, just before noon, as the church bells began to chime.

Phil's mother called Mrs. Hecht, and Mr. Hecht was waiting for his daughters outside the church when they got out at 12:10. Helen held Boots's hand as they walked home with their father. At home, after getting solemn hugs from her father and her brother Daniel, who heard about the death over his ham radio, Boots asked her mother if she could be excused from Sunday dinner. She went to her room. Shortly after one, Helen peeked into her room to see if she was all right, and Boots was gone.

Hiding under the autumn leaves in the ditch with her rifle, Boots listened to the men plan their search for her. Rowdy Bates declared the main area of the search would be around the quarry. Mr. Hecht and Daniel searched every spot they had ever taken Boots hunting. There was no sign of the girl.

Phil Anderson's funeral and burial were Tuesday, but Boots still had not been found. Mrs. Hecht made an unusual public appearance and sat in a pew behind Phil's mother. At least one town gossip said she saw Mrs. Hecht pat Mrs. Anderson on the shoulder twice during the service.

Wednesday morning, around 6:00 AM, Mrs. Hecht telephoned the sheriff's office to call off the search. Laura Mae had been found, asleep in her white canopy bed, the pink coverlet thrown on the floor, her doe-skin shirt crumpled in a bundle in her arms, her pillow still damp from her tears.

Rowdy Bates thanked Mrs. Hecht for calling, saying that he had to track down some vandals who were out doing Halloween pranks while he and his men were searching the quarry and the woods for Boots.

"What kind of pranks, Rowdy?" Mrs. Hecht asked.

"The usual. Someone shot out all the tires on Doc Stokowski's hearse, plus put two bullet holes in the weathervane on his house and three in his mailbox. And Mr. Schlemmer's store window was shattered with what appears to be a .22 rifle bullet."

"About everyone around here has a .22 rifle," Mrs. Hecht said, her voice oddly off pitch. "Do you have any idea who did it?" she asked.

"I'm not looking for anyone in Grafton," Rowdy reassured. "It was probably some Alton boys up here to get their kicks."

Mrs. Hecht's voice quickly returned to normal, calm, and sure as ever. "Hooligans. Some poor mother's torment."

Leaving
Central, IL — circa 1937

Jesus Christ! I guess I shouldn't have hit her so hard last night. It was the first time I ever hit her with my fist, but she deserved it—god dammit! She deserved it. She was always putting the kids before me. I told her to have my supper ready, and there she was in the kitchen drinking a cup a coffee, the table covered with Frank Jr.'s homework, and not a bite to eat in sight. I knocked that cup right out of her hand. "What the hell are you doing? Where's my supper?"

"Frank, honey, it's after 9:00. I figured you'd decided to eat out."

"And where the hell do you think I'd get the money to eat out?"

"I didn't think . . ."

"That's the problem, you never think!" She was looking at Frank Jr., motioning to him to get his stuff together, get it off the table, and I knew she was doing it more for him than me. "Let him be and get me something to eat. Now!"

She moved away, between me and the boy. I could see she was afraid for him, but it just made me madder. It was like I didn't count at all. My fist had busted her across the mouth before I knew I'd thrown the punch. Her upper lip began to swell, and blood ran down her chin, but she didn't cry out.

She just stood there, comforting Frank Jr., who had jumped up out of his chair and run to her. He was clinging to her side, and she was holding him to her. It was so pathetic. I took the dish towel by the sink, put some ice in it from the freezer, and handed it to her. She whimpered something to the boy then put the ice to her lip.

Later, after I ate the supper she heated up for me and she put the kids to bed, I told her I was sorry. She held my head in her lap and stroked my hair, the way she used to in the back seat of the old Ford when we were parked by the river. God! I had forgotten how much I loved her then.

When I first saw Laura Mae Hecht, she was sixteen. Her chest was flat and she had one of those bobbed haircuts. Wearing a man's flannel shirt and her jeans tucked into hiking boots, she looked more like a boy than a girl. She was by herself, leaning against the school yard fence and smoking a cigarette.

I wheeled the old Ford up to the curb and leaned across the front seat, beckoning for her to come over to the car. She just stood there like she didn't even see me. Me, Frank DeLano. The top of the charts with the girls in Grafton.

Two years later, I met her in the woods. She had just taken down a buck with a 30-06 deer rifle, a buck I had been trailing. Instead of taking her apart, the way I might have another guy in the same situation, I turned on the DeLano charm.

"You planning to drag that buck back out of the woods all by yourself, ma'am?" I said.

"I got help coming," she said. "My brother will be here soon. He must of heard the shot."

"I'm sure glad to hear you didn't come hunting out here all alone," I said.

"I don't see that's any of your business," she said.

"A pretty girl like you, I'd like to make my business."

"And how do you expect you can do that?" she said.

She was smiling that "You sure got a line, Mister" smile that girls use to mean, "I'm outta here."

"For starters, I'll help you and your brother get this deer out of the woods and back to town. Then I'd like to take you dancing next Saturday night." I could see she was about to say no. "You can't get another deer this season, so why not get out of the woods and into your dancing shoes?" I said.

"I don't even know you," she said.

"Well, you can ask around. You're going to hear that Frank DeLano is a great date."

"Frank DeLano." She seemed surprised, like she'd heard of me.

"Okay now, what's your name?"

"Laura Mae Hecht. Everyone calls me Boots."

"How about it, Laura Mae? Dancing next Saturday night?"

"I'll think about it," she said, just as her brother was coming into sight. "Call me."

I loved her as much as I loved any of them, but from our first date, she was lifetime crazy about me. Within three months we were going steady, except for a girlfriend I had who lived about thirty miles south in a little Jersey County town. I managed to get away to see her once or twice a month.

By the end of six months, Laura Mae was pregnant. My folks liked her, and I figured she would make a good enough wife. When old Farley at the gas station heard we were getting married, he gave me a raise up to thirty-five cents an hour and promised to make me a manager in two or three years.

We did pretty well at first, but I wasn't meant for settling down. The more domesticated she got, the more unhappy I got. I took to staying down at the station nights or going to a bar before I came home. Before the boy was a year old, I was running around on her. It's all lies about my not giving her enough money to buy food for the kids. I always gave her half my check for household expenses. I had to have my spending money.

By the time Frank Jr. was nine and Mae Ellen was seven, I was staying away as much as I was at home. When I did come home, I was usually drunk. Laura Mae was strong enough to take it. She just kept on being there, taking care of the kids, keeping my clothes clean and pressed, my bed warm, and the house going. She started reminding me of my mother, never saying much, hardly ever smiling.

This evening, just one night after I gave her that fat lip with my fist, she was at it again, feeding those damn kids when I wanted her to rub my back. I told her I was in a scuffle at the bar and needed a rubdown. She barely looked up. She smiled in that "butter wouldn't melt in her mouth" way she has, said, "Just a minute, Hon. I'll be right there. Don't want the kids pouring this hot soup, they might get burnt."

I showed her. Told her I was taking those little brats and dumping them with their grandma. The look on her face was fierce.

"You ain't taking my kids nowhere. Not now! Not anytime you've been drinking!" She stood straighter, firmer than any tree I've seen. "You go drink with your buddies or lay up with any whore you want, but you ain't taking my kids out of the house if you're drunk."

I grabbed Mae Ellen by the little lace collar on her dress and Frank Jr. by his belt loop and started dragging them right out to the car.

"I swear it, Frank. I'll get my rifle," Boots said, frantic.

"Go to hell, you bitch! I'll take my kids anywhere, anytime, I want."

Frank Jr. was fighting me, trying to get away, and Mae

Ellen was crying. God, I hate crying. I showed her the back of my hand and then she was kind of sniffling. I dragged them to the car and put them in the back seat. By the time I was behind the wheel, Laura Mae had her twenty-two raised up to her shoulder.

First shot took out the front left wheel, second one got the right. I knew she wouldn't shoot me. I started backing out of the driveway. Next thing I knew she was in the yard, shooting out the back tires. I braked and she rushed the back door of the car. She had the kids out of the car and heading across the field to the Ramsey's before I could get out to stop them.

"You bitch!" I shouted. "I'm leaving you forever this time." I kept backing that car down the driveway on flat tires. "And I'll get the brats, too. You can't stop me by shooting out the tires!"

I could see the kids still running across the field, Mae Ellen falling a bit behind; Frankie stumbling, turning, grabbing her hand, half dragging her over the stubble. I heard Laura Mae screaming, "Run, Frankie. Run! Don't let your sister fall." Turning to me, she yelled, "I won't let you have them, Frank DeLano."

Then she backed up onto the porch, reloaded that rifle, raised it to her shoulder, and I heard one last shot. I went numb, the top of my body flopped over, and I just sank right out of myself.

I heard her screaming, "No! No! God, I didn't mean to."

It was like I could see it all through her. Nothing was familiar any more though. The banging of the screen door, or was it more shots. No, shots are louder. All the people. Who in the hell were they? Where'd they come from? We seemed to know them, and then their faces all around us grew strange.

"Put it down! Put it down now. Please Boots!" Uncle Ralph was trying to get Laura Mae to put the rifle down. He used her nickname, pleading with her. She was holding the stock so tight her fingers were turning white.

A sheriff's deputy was coming closer, pistol raised.

Uncle Ralph knew he could get her to listen. "Put it down, Boots! What about the kids?"

Her eyes were wild, but she understood that. I was beginning to be able to read her mind. The kids. She had to take care of the kids. She let go of the gun. Uncle Ralph grabbed it in one hand and put his other arm around her to hold her up.

They were pulling my body out from behind the wheel of the car. My dad had hold of it under the arms. Once it was out of the car, my brother, Russell, took my legs. They brought my body up onto the porch, into the house and laid it on the couch, which got soaked with blood.

People were feeling my pulse, putting a mirror up to my mouth and nose. I could hear sirens getting closer and closer. Laura Mae pulled away from Ralph, pushed past my dad and brother, and kneeled beside the couch. She put her hand up to my cheek, rubbed it lightly, and began to stroke my hair.

"I just wanted to stop you." A long, low moaning sound. "You can't die, Frank. Please don't leave me!"

I wished that her wanting it could bring me back.

By now, I couldn't feel anything and my thoughts and hers were melded. She kneeled against the couch, her head on the cushion, sobbing and stroking my hair, my blood beginning to mat in her hair. I could feel a great emptiness growing inside her where the last of her love for me had been.

Lies and Consequences
Alton, IL — circa 1948

My grandmother used "the gypsies" as a threat to make me mind. They were the ones who took bad little girls away and never brought them back. When I stayed at my grandmother's house, she would say, "Don't go out of the yard. If you go far from the yard, the gypsies will get you."

When we went to the corner market, she would hold my hand so tightly in her knobby grasp that it hurt. I would squirm and try to wriggle away from her, "Grandma, you're hurting me."

"Better to be hurt by your grandmother than to have gypsies get you," she would say. I was quite terrified of gypsies. I asked my mother where the gypsies lived and why I never saw any gypsy children at school.

"There are no gypsies in Alton," she said in a tone that added "foolish girl" to her answer.

Angry that my mother thought me foolish, I blurted out, "Grandma Hecht talks about them all the time. Is she lying?"

Even as I said this, I felt ashamed. I felt almost as if I'd said damn or Hell. Telling a lie was one of the worst things you could do in our household. It was next to stealing, and I was accusing my mother's mother of doing this terrible thing.

My mother turned her head away from the dishes so quickly, I thought for an instant it might break off at the neck. Her right hand leapt out of the sink with soapy water all over it and suds dripping to the linoleum floor. I thought she was going to slap me. I was so startled that I began to cry. I tried to hold back my tears, but they came anyway.

"What has gotten into to you, Sissy? A seven-year-old girl accusing her grandmother of lying!"

My mother's face was fire red. I began to back away. Then she wiped a wisp of blonde hair back from her forehead with the soap sudsy hand and sighed.

She pulled me to her and held me tightly, my face pushed against her soiled apron. Patting my back gently with her wet hand, still warm from the hot dishwater, she ran her fingers through my hair. She comforted me as if I were a baby, then added, "You mustn't be disrespectful of your grandma."

I had heard Mother and her sister be disrespectful of Grandma. Once they were laughing about how she used to chase their friends with a broom.

"How many kids have a real witch for a mother?" Aunt Boots said. "Remember how scared everyone was of our house on Halloween? What a hoot!"

They laughed again. My mother didn't know I heard them, and I knew this was not the time to mention their disrespect. Still, I stubbornly pursued the gypsy issue.

"But Grandma's always telling me the gypsies will get me. Why does she do that if there aren't any?"

My mother's face did not turn red and angry again. "There were gypsies where your grandma grew up."

"Did they steal little kids like Grandma says?"

"I don't think so, but I'm sure Grandma's mother told her they did."

"Your grandma told lies, too!" I felt like this must be the bad seed in our family.

"Yes, I guess so. Little white lies." Then Mother smiled at me the way she always did just before she said, "You'll understand someday," but she didn't say it.

"What are white lies?" I persisted.

"They are lies you tell that don't hurt anyone."

I don't know why I didn't question her more. I suppose something, or someone, interrupted us. Years later, when Grandmother Hecht lived with us, I sometimes heard her screaming in the night. Doors would open and slam shut. I would hear mother's running feet in floppy slippers, slapping the hardwood floors, rushing to my grandmother's room.

Often, between the opening and shutting of doors, I could hear my grandmother's frightened screams. "The gypsies, they're coming. Please don't let them take me. Help me! HELP ME! The gypsies are coming."

I hid under the stairs and wished I had a secret place where Grandma would feel safe.

The Intruder
Alton, IL — 1950s

The tall, gangly, fifty-five-year-old Kentuckian with the slow drawl of his home state and the soft eyes of an innocent first spoke to Boots in the plant cafeteria line. To speak without being introduced was completely out of character for him, but he raised his work hat and said, "How do, Ma'am?"

"How do, yourself, Mr. Macon," Boots snapped.

Her amused smile and the fact that she knew his name surprised him. Thinking she was pleased that he spoke, he blundered on, because the only women he ever spoke to besides his wife and daughters were the ladies of his church, for whom he often did handyman's chores. He told her the one thing about him that seemed of most importance to them.

"I'm pretty good with my hands ma'am."

Boots looked at him with such a scowl that he realized the double meaning and blushed like a child.

"I mean, I'm good at fixing things. I can fix most anything you need fixed."

"I see," she said.

"I just wonder if you have any work for a handyman, Ma'am."

They were at the cash register now. Boots was getting coins out of a circular leather coin purse that was folded down at the edge with each fold lying over the next so that when you squeezed it, it opened, and when you released it, it closed, spiraling in and holding shut. Boots looked at it and thought of how her life was spiraling in on her and holding her shut.

"Will you let me buy your coffee?" Macon asked, making a signal with his long fingers for her to put her money away.

"You're buying?" she said.

"I'd like that," he said.

"Sure, but have the girl at the counter hand me a piece of that lemon pie too, Macon. I didn't realize how hungry I was."

Everybody called him by his last name, Macon, since his first name, Americus was so unusual. Macon suited him though. People who met him always had the same impression—that he was from the deep South—and connected him with Macon, Georgia.

"Please get the lady a piece of lemon pie," Macon said to the girl behind the serving table. Boots had not been called a lady in a long time. "And get one of those big pieces of pecan pie for me, please," he said.

Boots just stood there, watching him. After paying, he picked up her tray in one hand and his in the other and motioned for her to move out into the lunchroom. As they stepped away from the counter, some of the other men from the production line started whistling and hooting.

A heavyset woman with a pudgy pink hand, grabbed Boots's work smock and sneered, "Watch it, missy. His old lady may be a slut, but she sure packs a wallop."

Boots sneered back and walked on. Half a lunchroom later she sat down on the shiny gray bench, glad that the whistles and jeers had stopped and that the only sounds now were the loud hum of conversation, the clicking of silverware on stoneware, and the whir of the heavy-duty ceiling fan above their heads. Neither spoke for a while, both tackling their desserts the way people who have short breaks do.

"Well," he said. "Do you have anything that needs fixing?"

My whole life, thought Boots, but she answered, "No."

"You sure? Everybody's house needs some fixing."

"What makes you think I have a house?"

Puzzled, Macon sat a minute. "If you don't, you should." He smiled. "A nice lady like you."

There's that lady stuff again, Boots thought. He's too much. She pushed the last bite of her pie aside and got up with a force that surprised her and shook the gray wood bench. "Well, I don't, and I'll thank you to forget using your hands to fix anything for me!"

Macon watched her hurry across the lunchroom to whistles and cat calls. Then he ate the rest of his pie and the last bite of hers, too.

Two days later, Boots and Helen discussed the encounter with Macon over a cup of Helen's boiling hot, black coffee. Since it was her day off, Boots had slept until 10:30, lying in her bed upstairs another forty-five minutes, reading a Frank Yerby novel. Helen always let Boots sleep. This was one of the reasons they were all able to live in the same house.

Helen's family lived downstairs, while Boots and their older sister, Philomena, who everyone called Aunt Phil, each had rooms upstairs in the white two-story house on the corner of Edwards and Clausen Streets.

The house's yard and flower gardens were the pride of the neighborhood. The centerpiece was a Japanese Quince bush in the front yard that towered a foot above the porch roof and was as big around as a carnival merry-go-round. After its leaves turned completely red, people driving by would often stop to admire it from the street. It was good that the bush was in front, for Grandma Hecht, who owned the house with

Philomena and lived in a two-room mother-in-law apartment on the east side of the house, would have been unsettled if she knew that their house had become a center of attention in the neighborhood.

Helen and her family moved in because someone had to be with Grandma Hecht, and Helen, unlike Philomena and Boots, did not work outside the home, except for part-time work as a democratic precinct committee woman that brought her a small amount of money of her own. Thus, it was Helen and Joe Wasilec who were there to take care of Boots's children, Mae Ellen and Frankie, during years when their mother was unable to care for them financially or emotionally. All this was made possible by Philomena, who was a schoolteacher and made a good enough living, along with Grandma Hecht's widow's pension, to support herself, the house, and Grandma Hecht.

Helen and Boots divided the responsibilities of the house according to their individual talents. Helen did all the housework and cooking while Boots took care of Grandma Hecht's personal care, washing and ironing her clothes, and her shopping, just as she had done when she was a teenager, thirty years before.

Helen also took care of the finances and the yard. She had emerged from the dumb blonde model she adopted in high school to have a great head for finance. Boots handled their mother's more and more frequent fits of senility, looking under the bed for burglars and chasing away the gypsies who Grandma Hecht feared had come to get her. This happened several times a week, between the hours of midnight and six in the morning.

Philomena had no responsibilities around the house other than cleaning her own room upstairs, keeping up the payments, and providing Helen and Boots with a monthly allotment of money to spend for their mother's food and personal needs.

When she was invited, Aunt Phil would come downstairs to eat dinner with Helen's family. She especially liked Helen's pork roast, which was served with mashed potatoes and gravy, homemade dinner rolls, and Helen's famous wilted lettuce, which made the whole house smell of fresh fried bacon. On these special evenings, Aunt Phil would always wash the dishes before going back upstairs to prepare her lesson for the next day and read her Bible.

"Sounds like a pretty nice fellow to me," Helen said. "Must be dumb as owl shit though."

"Why?"

"Calling you a lady." Helen laughed.

"Well, maybe so," Boots laughed too. "He sure looks dumb, all cow-eyes, looking at me like I'm something special."

"What's his name?" Helen asked.

"Macon."

"From Georgia?"

"No, everyone thinks he is, but he's really from Dover, Kentucky. He came up here twenty-three years ago with a teenage bride and a baby. Now he's got three grown daughters and a wife who runs around on him."

You've been asking around about him." Helen pointed her finger at Boots and shook her head, which was already tied in a scarf for cleaning. "I thought you weren't interested."

"I'm not, just curious."

"Well, I am interested," Helen said. "You can get yourself a decent guy for a change, and we can get some work done around this place." Helen's face shone with excitement. "I'm going to start him on Mom's sink. I'm tired of lugging the pan of water from that leak in the drainpipe."

"If you think I'm going to go out with a hillbilly so you can get a drainpipe fixed, you're dumber than he is!"

Within a week, Macon was fixing the drainpipe under Grandma Hecht's sink. Helen had to admit that he seemed slow-witted because everything he said and did was done at the pace of a southern drawl, an annoyance because she was used to a less leisurely approach to her work.

It was Helen who had searched him out and told him of their need of a handyman. "My husband can't hang a picture, Mr. Macon. Boots says you come highly recommended."

"Call me, Macon, Ma'am," he said, his smile reflecting his pleasure at Boots's compliment.

Of course, Boots had said no such thing, but one of Helen's most useful traits was knowing what people wanted to hear and saying it, whether it was true or not.

"A little white lie," Helen would tell her daughter, Sis, "sometimes accomplishes so much more than the truth. And if it's a white lie, nobody gets hurt."

Boots found Macon's frequent presence at the kitchen table drinking coffee with Helen annoying. Morning after morning when she got up late after working midnights, or working afternoons and drinking into the early AM, Boots would wake up to the smell of fresh coffee and the sound of muffled voices coming from the kitchen. The heat shafts in the gravity-based heat system connected the kitchen and her upstairs bedroom. "God damn it to Hell anyway," she would mutter under her breath. "A person doesn't have any privacy in this house."

One Saturday morning, to spite them, Boots deliberately skipped her traditional morning toilet, including brushing her teeth or combing her hair. She put on a tattered, chenille robe, and left her thin hair untouched and in curlers so that it stuck up out in several directions. Still, when she reached the kitchen table, which had been their mother's—a relic of life in Pennsylvania with its porcelain top decorated with Pennsylvania Dutch figures and wood carved trim on metal legs—Macon stood and pulled a chair out for her, his big, love-struck eyes watching for some sign that her feelings for him were warming up.

Helen walked over to the stove and returned with the battered metal coffee pot and a china cup with yellow roses on it. Boots recognized it as one of the most recent sets that Helen had gotten from a grocery store promotion. She could not repress a smile at the sight of her sister, every blonde hair in place, wearing a freshly washed and pressed house dress, with a freshly washed and pressed apron, ruffled and tied in a bow, serving coffee in a sunshiny, sparkling clean kitchen. Helen looked like an advertisement for some new product.

"Would you like an egg?" Helen asked. "Macon brought some over, fresh from the chicken farm at Hamel. Wasn't that sweet?"

"White or brown shell?" Boots asked.

"Brown," Macon answered, turning to Helen. "Helen likes brown country eggs."

"Well, Helen knows I don't like anything country," Boots said, looking straight at her sister.

"I know better than that, Miss Boots," Macon said. "You like the country pies they have at the plant cafeteria."

"Toast," Boots growled at Helen. "Just toast." Getting up from the table, she walked to the refrigerator and opened the door. "Do we have any tomato juice?" she asked, rummaging through the well-packed shelves.

"In the Halls pitcher with the fall leaves on it," Helen replied.

Boots smiled. The Halls pitcher was another premium Helen had received for buying a certain amount of goods from the Jewell Tea salesman. *This house is chock full of crap like this,* Boots thought, lifting the heavy china pitcher. "What about Tabasco?"

"In the door," Helen said, sitting down, discouraged for the first time that morning. "Is that all you're going to eat? Toast and tomato juice with Tabasco?"

"Great combination to beat a hangover."

Macon also had a discouraged look on his face. He was stirring a third spoonful of sugar into his coffee. Helen's coffee was, as she told visitors, "Strong enough to walk on its own."

Macon always drank it with lots of milk and sugar. He was thinking that he would get Helen some country cream the next trip he took to Hamel when Boots's voice interrupted. "Will you stop that infernal clinking!"

Macon dropped the spoon as if it were hot. Coffee splashed over the edge of the cup. Macon leapt to his feet to keep the coffee from splashing on him, and his chair fell over and banged against the counter.

Boots started laughing, then Helen, then somewhat less enthusiastically, Macon. As he sat back down, they were each quiet for a short while until Helen spoke. "Macon has offered to take us to the movies this afternoon, then out to supper at the Uptown Diner."

"He has?" Boots said.

"Yes ma'am, I have." Macon said.

"And who is us?" Boots asked, knowing the answer but stretching the moment as far she could.

"Why, you, Miss Boots, and Miss Helen here, and little Sis."

This was Helen's standard trick, to invite Macon to do something with them or get him to invite them to do something that Boots could not refuse, like taking her niece to a Saturday afternoon matinee.

"I wish you would stop making plans for me," Boots said, looking at Helen for the second time that morning with real anger in her eyes. "Have you already told Sis?" Boots knew Helen had, so her nodded yes was unnecessary, but it was part of their ritual. "How would you feel if I had to work, and you had to disappoint Sis?" Boots said.

"But you don't," Helen said. "I looked at your schedule. You're off till Monday."

"So you've planned my whole damned weekend I suppose!" Boots stood up, slamming the table with her cup.

Helen looked hurt, and Macon looked startled. Helen had assured him that Boots loved going to the movies and eating out afterwards. She also had suggested stopping at the soda fountain on the way home because Boots loved chocolate sundaes.

Looking at them both, Boots knew she had lost. The only way to beat them was to not come home at all, and since her failed relationship with a local bar owner that she lived with off and on for several years, she had no place else to go. "Wake me in time to get ready."

"You'll go?" Helen and Macon both asked at once.

"Yes."

"Sis will be so happy," Helen said.

Boots knew it was true. Sis was beginning to live for the times they all went out together, and Helen too. Joe Sr. was never home, and when he was home, he never paid much attention to Helen or Sis. He usually just sat by the radio, or television—the first one in the neighborhood—listening to sports, smoking cigars, and reading the newspapers. Macon always managed to pay attention to all three of them. He never complained about how much anything cost, and he never seemed to be in a hurry to go home.

Most important to Helen and Sis was that their excursions with Boots and Macon never ended in the ritual arguments that family times with Joe Sr. did. The regular fights became so frequent that Helen looked forward to Joe being away from home. Everyone knew Joe had, not one, but several women on the side. Helen didn't care as long as it kept him away from her.

Boots disliked Joe for all the grief she felt he brought to Helen's life. She gave him one credit though. Joe had been very good to her children when they lived with him and Helen.

Macon courted Boots for six months before she started accepting him in their lives. In that time, he became an ever-present member of the household. The neighbors were beginning to talk about the possibility of a romance, not between Boots and Macon, but between Helen and Macon.

Helen didn't care. She enjoyed having Macon around. He would do anything for her to be near Boots, and Helen took full advantage of this. Macon repaired the plumbing under two kitchen sinks and two bathroom sinks. He replaced three screens on the big front porch, reinforced the steps on the back porch, reroofed the shed next to the garage, put new doors on two of the kitchen cabinets, and built a new cabinet over the stove. This required refinishing the old ones, which Macon happily did. Then, she started him working in the flower gardens. All of these things were accomplished with the cheery disposition of a happy child who knows that if he's good Santa Claus will reward him at Christmastime.

At first Boots rebelled against her sister's manipulation of their lives. She also didn't like the way Helen took advantage of Macon. Then she realized that even thinking this sympathetic thought was a sign that the process was working. She had changed from total disdain of Macon to a type of empathy.

Boots and Helen talked about how they both felt they were their mother's and older sister's victims, forced to live communally the way they did, but now Boots was feeling that she was Helen's victim.

Boots was not an alcoholic, but she drank too much to be her mother's only guardian, too much for her to care for her children during their teenage years, too much to care if her last boyfriend knocked her around a bit and her last husband cheated at cards, and too much for her to sleep at night after work unless she drank some more.

She never drank at home alone, only in bars, or parked cars, or men's places.

She also never drank too much in front of Sis. The young girl depended on Boots to counterweight Helen's demands for perfection. She counted on Aunt Boots to give her books Helen would not let her read—like *The Saracen Blade* by Frank Yerby—the book that made Sis's young body squirm when she read the love scenes.

Boots also defended Sis when Helen berated the teenager for reading and studying too much or wasting time writing stories and poems.

"Writing stories never hurt me when I was growing up," Boots said.

"You think you're a good role model?" Helen said. "Didn't do you much good either, did it?" The words could have come right out of Grandma Hecht's mouth.

Boots and Sis got along quite well. "We have to be, buddies," Boots would say. "We both need a buddy, living in this crazy house with the whole damned family."

Thank god my kids and Joe Jr. were out of here before I moved in. Laura Mae was glad they were grown and away before she was forced to come back and live with her family like a child who could not take care of herself. Boots tried to answer all Sis's questions truthfully, no matter what she asked.

"When I grow up, do you think I will hate sex the way Mama does?" Sis said.

"No one else could hate sex as much as your mama does," Boots said. She did not add that from what Helen had told Boots, having sex with Joe Sr. was like being raped every night. "Sex feels good, you'll like it. Men feel good inside you, and sometimes they fill up the emptiness."

"What emptiness?" Sis said.

"Any emptiness," Boots said, not wanting to explain more.

Sis stood there with a puzzled look on her face, more questions in her eyes, the same blue as Boots's, the same blue as her mother's, Helen's. She would not ask anyone else in the family what Aunt Boots meant because Helen told her daughter never to repeat anything her Aunt Boots said.

Boots often went over to the bar across the street from the plant right after work. First, she took a shower in the women's shower room, fluffed up her curly, reddish-blonde hair in the front over her forehead, combed back the sides, and then fluffed up the short curls in back. She put a little make-up on—powder, rouge, and the bright red lipstick that was in style. Boots loved anything bright red.

She sniffed under her chemise to see if she had gotten the plant smell off—the sulfurous odor of Southern Illinois coal burning. Before she put on the fresh white blouse and brown slacks she had hanging in her locker, she sprayed White Shoulders cologne over the upper part of her body. Stuffing the cologne in her bag, in case the plant smell was still with her, she slammed the locker shut, turned the combination lock, and headed up the stairs to the tunnel.

Boots always took the tunnel under the street with a couple of the other women on the shift and several of the men. Everyone was usually in high spirits, just off work and ready for a good time. Boots liked the sound of their voices and footsteps bouncing off the walls and echoing through the tunnel. When the traffic growled and rumbled above, Boots imagined that she was in an exciting city, heading into the subway, waiting for a train that would take her far away from Owens Illinois Glass and her life, but take her where? That was the problem with Boots's dreams of getting away, she had no particular place in mind.

When Joe Sr. was on the same shift as Boots and was walking with the other men in the group, there was no sense in pretending she didn't see him, so she would yell up the line, "Hey Joe, if I get smashed tonight, will you take me home?" It was a game they played. Everyone in the group knew he was her brother-in-law and the family's living arrangement.

"Why can't you call that big Kentucky mule of yours, Macon, to come get you?" Joe would call back.

"Cause he's home fixing something for your wife."

Then everyone would laugh, and only Joe Sr. and Boots would know the real joke, that this was true. If Macon was off, he was at their house. In fact, Macon spent more time at the big white house on Edwards St. than Boots or Joe Sr.

The teasing had begun one night when Boots actually had gotten smashed enough to have to ask Joe Sr. to take her home.

"Joe, why don't you ever complain about Macon spending so much time at the house?" Boots said, her left arm around his neck, his right arm around her waist, so he could help her walk to the car.

"I guess for the same reason Helen doesn't complain about you and me drinking in the same joints."

"You mean because she knows we hate each other."

"More because Helen doesn't really enjoy sex. She would give him the boot if he tried anything."

"Damn right." Boots was having a hard time remembering what they were even talking about. "Where's the car?"

Joe pointed across the street in the plant lot. "Helen is just being nice to that dumbass southerner."

"My sister, the saint."

"But she's practical," Joe laughed. "She's nice to them, and they're nice to her. She gets a lot of things she wants that way."

Boots thought about that a moment, thinking it strange that Joe Sr. knew this about Helen. She wasn't sure anyone else did. "So you don't think my sister is making it with my boyfriend, who isn't my boyfriend?"

"What?" Joe said.

"My boyfriend who isn't!"

"You're drunk."

"No! Really. You catch on quick."

"You are talking like a damned drunk now."

"Well, I am a damned drunk. "

Boots was not surprised that Joe Sr. believed that Macon and she were an item. Everyone in their household did, including Macon. The only one that still believed they weren't was Boots herself. *How I let this happen,* she thought. *It pleases Helen so much, having him around, fixing things. Now he's helping her with the flower gardens. I let on that I liked him enough to keep him coming back. I'm just as damned manipulative as Helen.*

There was no doubt Macon had become a fixture in the family, an encroaching presence in Boots's life. She felt like the house was a glass ant farm anyway. It amused her to think of God watching them all, working away in their own crawl spaces, but with Macon there all the time. She began to feel suffocated, like her crawl space was crumbling and plugging up.

Three weeks to the day after Macon filed for divorce, Boots ran into one of her old boyfriends in the bar. "How's it going with that Kentucky Mule of yours, Boots?"

"None of your business," Boots said, slurring the words so much that even she realized she had probably hit her limit.

"We were just wondering, such a small woman, and him being so big, and all."

"Huh? "Boots looked up at him. "What are you getting at?"

"Now Boots, when I knew you, you were pretty tight— from what some guys have seen of Macon in the shower, I bet you're stretched a bit now?"

Boots swirled around on the bar stool, the drink in her hand, and smacked her tormenter in the side of the face. The glass broke in her hand, cutting her, not him. He made a quick exit while the bartender hurried around the side of the bar to help Boots. After wrapping her hand in a bar towel, he helped her to the back where he ran it under the cold-water faucet in the sink. The cut was small, but he bandaged it anyway.

"Get me another seven and seven!" Boots said.

"No, I'm calling your folks. You need to go home now. What's the number."

"Howard, 2-5-0-7-9. Thanks."

Boots, waiting at a table where she could see the street, wasn't surprised to see Macon's old green Pontiac pull up and stop. She took a last sip of the coffee the bartender had given her.

Macon got out of the car and came in after her. He put his long arm around her shoulders and held her close to him so she would not fall. She realized that she had never let him hold her before, even like this.

On the drive home, he tried to make small talk, but she just sat there, wondering how she had gone from her first love—a tall, good-looking young man who died on her—to the crude sort like the one she had smacked tonight.

Why, I can't want someone like you, she thought, looking at Macon. Although his face was long and thin, he was nice enough looking. Boots usually liked more boyish men. *How many men are boyish looking pushing fifty-six? I'm lucky he doesn't want someone girlish looking.* This was her last thought before she passed out with her head on Macon's shoulder.

When they got to the house at 12:10 AM, Helen took over. She told Macon to get a cup of coffee and wait for her in the kitchen. Joe Sr. wasn't in yet. Philomena was asleep; and once she was out for the night, she was out for the night. Grandma Hecht had gone to bed easily that night, and Sis was sleeping over at a friend's house. Helen noted that getting Boots to bed was the last thing she had to do that day.

After helping Boots to the bathroom, changing her bandage, and getting her into her flannel pajamas, Helen put her to bed. Boots wore pajamas because she didn't like to be around the house with Joe Sr. in gowns. She wore flannel because the upstairs was always a little cool. Tonight, the flannel comforted her somehow, its softness soothing her, making her feel loved and cared for. Helen was making her feel loved and cared for.

"Why are you combing my hair?" Boots asked.

"I thought it would make you feel better." Helen answered. "I remember when we used to comb each other's hair a hundred strokes at night."

"Did we? I don't remember," Boots was still groggy.

"Yes, and then I combed Mae Ellen's, and Sis's, but Sis won't let me anymore." As soon as Boots dozed off, Helen tucked the covers around her and went downstairs to Macon.

"She looks so pretty now, Macon. You should see her." Helen seemed to be talking to herself. "I combed her hair for her. It looked like she hadn't combed it all day."

"She's a mighty pretty woman when she keeps herself nice," Macon replied. "But she doesn't do that very often anymore."

"I know, she just doesn't seem to know where she's going or what she's doing. She needs a good man like you to help her through." Helen smiled. "She told me you were so gentle with her tonight, that she just wanted to kiss you and thank you, but she was too ashamed."

"She doesn't have to feel ashamed."

"Well, she is." Helen got up from her chair, walked over behind Macon, and started rubbing his back. "And she knows about your wife being such a slut, too," Helen said. She was rubbing his shoulders hard, then putting her thumbs together on the back of his neck and pressing gently, moving up his neck and back down to his shoulders. "She feels like she's not good enough for you."

It had been more than a year since Macon had been touched by a woman, other than a few furtive kisses he gave Boots and the quick hugs and kisses that Helen gave him from time to time to thank him for a job well done. His body began to react to the back rub to a point that was quite noticeable even through his loose work pants. Finally, he pulled forward, away from her.

"Stop! My back feels just fine now."

"Does it Macon?" Helen said. Walking around in front of him.

"Yes, Ma'am. I'd better be getting home now."

Helen was standing so that he couldn't get up without bumping into her. "Macon, do you really want to go home?" Helen said. "Wouldn't you rather sleep over here tonight?"

"What?"

"I know it's been a long time since you've been with a woman, but don't you think you could get it all back?" Helen was bending down toward him, rubbing the front of his shoulders, her breath as she talked touching his neck and his ears. "I bet you could get it all back, and there's nobody to wake up now. Joe Sr. won't be back for hours."

Macon stood up, backing away from her as quickly as possible without too much contact between his and her body.

"You need a woman, Macon, and there's a woman in this house that needs you," Helen said.

If Macon's unsophisticated mind had been less clouded by his trust in Helen and what he believed was her selfless commitment to the whole family's best interest, but most especially his and Boots's, he might have been less confused by his body's reaction to Helen's onslaught.

Macon bent down to Helen and kissed her on the mouth. Helen responded with a light kiss.

"Can we?" Macon asked, his mind foundering, "Can we make love, Boots?"

Helen pushed him away a bit and looked up at him, her blue eyes full of promise, "That's right Macon. You don't want me. It's Boots you want."

"But she's upstairs asleep."

"She'll wake up when she feels you in bed with her," Helen said.

"Oh, no. I couldn't get in bed with her, not without her telling me it was all right."

"I'm telling you it's all right." Helen was leading him to the stairs, talking in a confident tone. "When she wakes up and finds you kissing and caressing her, she'll know it's right, too."

• • •

Boots rolled over in her bed, thinking she heard footsteps on the stairs. She lifted her head up a minute to look around, but there was nothing. More asleep than awake, still groggy from her night of drinking, she assured herself that it could not be an intruder. Someone would have heard him break in before he got all the way upstairs to her room.

She was slipping down further into her covers when she felt his hands on her. She started to pull away, but he was rolling her over.

"Boots, I love you," he was saying, "I need to make love to you." He was pulling the covers away from her and tugging at her pajama bottoms. She felt as if a mountain was lying on her.

"No, stop! What are you doing?"

He was leaning in to kiss her, but she was struggling. "You'll see. We'll get married." He used one hand to hold her still, "It will be alright then."

"You've gone crazy!"

Boots was still struggling. She shook her head to get the fogginess out of her brain. "Okay, Macon." A breath. "Okay." Another breath. "Yes, I might marry you. Just stop."

He couldn't stop himself.

This isn't happening. This couldn't be happening, again. Macon was on top of her, holding her down with one hand and unzipping his pants with the other. *How many times do I have to take this just because I am too friendly, or let myself trust the wrong man, in the wrong place? Enough! But this was Macon.*

He was on her, breathing like something wild. She was pushing at his face, trying to get him away. For whole minutes, she couldn't breathe. Finally, it was over.

Her mouth freed, she heard her own voice again, coming from outside her body, but hers, "What makes you think?" Breath. "Why?" Breath and sob. "How could you do this to me?"

He had released her but did not get up. She moved as far away from him on the bed as she could and turned away.

"Why Macon?" she asked again, her face turned away.

"Helen said I could . . . that you wouldn't mind." His voice was sounding less and less sure. "She promised me you wouldn't mind."

Boots lay still beside him, silent. *Helen said he could. God! When she thinks she's right, she's relentless . . . but this?*

Totally sapped, body and mind, Boots did not even have the strength to fight when Macon placed his arm over her body and curled himself around her. She had no strength to resist, or respond, or think, or care.

The wall she faced, devoid of color in the darkness, was an unexpected comfort; it offered a blank page, forgetfulness, sleep. *That's what I need, sleep. I drank too much and had a nightmare. Tomorrow morning, I won't remember; just like Mama forgets the gypsies.*

No Colored Wanted Here

Alton, IL — 1950s

"We're only talking about one colored child for a whole school." Helen Wasilec's voice was firm, but anxious. "Because I get out their vote, doesn't mean I'm the only person that should go."

Sis got out of bed, put on her fluffy pink slippers, and scuffed out to the dining room where her mother stood at the phone. She knew something was up. Instead of a clean house dress and apron, Helen was fully dressed in her navy-blue suit with the white cloth buttons that were circled in brass. A bright red lace-topped handkerchief was carefully placed in her left breast pocket. She was still in her nylon stocking feet, with her red leather purse and pumps sitting on the dining room table. The pumps were freshly cleaned and shined. This was Helen's only dressy outfit, and she kept it in mint condition, except for the tiny, imperceptible ash holes in the skirt, a reminder of Helen's chain smoking.

"I already told you I'm going over there," Helen said to the caller, her voice was accusatory now. "Especially since no one else plans to show up."

"Mama, what's wrong?" Sis said.

"Shush," Helen spoke into the phone without looking at her. "I think I met the mother once when I was working on your last campaign. She had some neighbors for a coffee. I remember there was a picture of Franklin Roosevelt on the wall of the living room. The house was spotless, not like I expected at all."

"Who has a picture of President Roosevelt on her wall?" Sis asked.

Still not looking at Sis, Helen waved her away with her cigarette hand, waving so close that the girl jumped back a bit to avoid the flying ashes. "Coloreds have as much right to a good education as anyone." There was silence. Helen's face was contorted with anger. "I don't care about stigmas on the precinct committee." Another silence. "We can't keep going into their neighborhoods and asking them to vote democratic if we can't let one colored child come into Horace Mann School."

That was the last word. Helen always got the last word, even if the other person did not realize it.

Sis was still standing close enough to hear, and she said, "Mama, will the colored child that's coming to school be as dark as Sambo in my old book?" She used her mother's word, "child," as if it were sacred, like the Christ child in the nativity scene at Christmas.

• • •

Helen was frustrated that Sis was still confused about "colored people." Just last summer, when Helen and Sis were walking uptown to the grocery store, Helen pointed to the side of a stone house at the corner of Clausen Street and College Avenue. The ground sloped down from the front of the house, exposing a part of the basement where an opening, smaller than a door but larger than a window, had been. It was closed in with white stones and cement.

"That's one of the stopping places where runaway slaves stayed," Helen said, pointing to the cemented place in the basement wall. As the democratic precinct committeewoman, Helen was proud of Upper Alton's heritage. "It was called the underground railroad."

"Where are the tracks?" nine-year-old Sis asked. Earlier in the summer, she had ridden on the Gulf, Mobile, and Ohio railroad to Chicago with her mother to see an aunt.

"There are no tracks, Sis!"

"It would be more fun if it was a real railroad with trains running under our houses."

"The underground railroad is just an expression for a way out of the southern states, hiding places for colored slaves trying to get free."

"Why did they call the slaves colored?"

"Because they're dark-skinned, not white, like us."

"We're not white, paper is white."

Impatient with Sis's constant questions, Helen started on up the street, pulling her daughter by the hand. "It's just a saying. Come on now. We have to get the groceries and be home in time to make supper for your Dad."

• • •

Helen was impatient with Sis this October morning, too.

"Sissy, go get dressed. You can't dawdle today. We have to get to school early!"

"You're going with me to school?" They lived across the street from the school, less than a minute's walk. Helen had not walked Sis to school since the child's first year at Horace Mann when she was in kindergarten.

"Yes, and we have to get moving." Helen kept talking as they headed into Sis's room.

"Why?" Sissy said.

"Why what?" Helen said, automatically starting to pick up the day-old clothes from the floor by the bed and putting them into a pink hamper that matched the rest of the pink decor, Helen's idea of a perfect girl's room.

"Why are you going, too? Is there going to be a party because the colored child is coming?"

"Not quite," Helen said. She looked worriedly at her unsuspecting daughter. "Most people are upset about this. I don't have time to explain. Come get your breakfast."

Sissy padded into the large, warm kitchen and sat at the end of the long, white enameled, wooden kitchen table that had recently replaced the old one from Pennsylvania. Helen sat a steaming bowl of Cream of Wheat in front of Sis and went into the bathroom.

"Is Mrs. Kolbert going to be at school, too?" Sis called after her.

"I don't know," Helen was putting on lipstick and combing her hair. "I don't even know if Carole will be there. Helen waved her cigarette filled hand again.

"Carole's not going to school! Can I stay home?" Sis did so well in school that Helen occasionally let her stay home when she wasn't sick. It was Sis's treat for getting straight A's.

"No, not today, especially not today!"

Mother and daughter entered the heavy steel front doors of the school at 7:00 AM, an hour early, but the halls were filling up with children and parents. The loud chorus of excited voices that usually sang through the halls in the morning had changed to a low rumble, indistinct and out of place.

George Grayson had a light beard still showing on his cheeks, as if he had not shaved that morning. He stepped up to talk quietly in Helen's ear as she stood just inside the door.

"Glad you're here, Mrs. Wasilec," he said. "Maybe you can tell the principal how we feel about this colored kid going to school with our kids."

"And how *do* we feel, Mr. Grayson?" Helen said.

"Like everyone does. That we don't want any coloreds in our school."

"Everyone, George," Helen said. *Just like you to be against this*, she thought, *such an average man.* "Did you take a poll?"

"You were at the PTA meeting last week. You saw how upset everyone was."

"I did, yes, and I was the one who moved to adjourn that useless meeting. It seems simple to me. The law is the law."

"But I thought that's why you were coming today."

"Did I give that impression? I hardly think so." She straightened to her full five feet two inches.

"Well, I'll be damned. You don't intend to support us, do you? You're going to stand with that nig . . . that colored woman over there, aren't you?"

Grayson went back to the group and Helen caught bits and pieces of the conversation, though they were trying not to be heard.

"I'll pull my kids out of school before I'll let them sit next to a colored."

"That's right," a woman just in front of Helen said quietly. This woman had never offered an opinion before on any topic. Helen was startled that she was even there.

Helen took Sis's hand and started walking away from the group. An olive-skinned woman with shining dark hair and a walnut-brown-skinned boy with steel wool curly hair sat outside the principal's office on the folding chairs that were for students waiting to be disciplined. Sis looked at them hard. She had never seen anyone so dark as the boy before. The two chairs next to them were vacant, and the crowd, a dozen parents, mothers and fathers, stood watching.

Helen had taught Sis never to stare, but the young girl could not help herself. She had never seen a negro up close. There were some that lived near her Grandma Wasilec's house, which sat back from the sidewalk of a large double corner lot. When negros walked by, they always stayed on the other side of the street.

"His mother must let that boy drink a lot of coffee!" Sis said, staring in the direction of the pair.

"Sis, what ARE you talking about?"

"Grandma Wasilec said I couldn't have coffee because it would make my skin turn black. He's got real black skin."

Some snickers from the parents' group bounced off the green and gray tiled walls of the foyer, and down to the hard tiled floors. All the tile and the bright fluorescent lighting made the hall seem colder than it was. The chilling blue-white artificial light shone on familiar faces, making them look unfamiliar, adding to the threatening atmosphere Helen felt all around her.

The boy's mother was not amused by Sis's remark. She held the boy's hand tighter and sat up even straighter on the hard wooden chair. She was dressed neatly in a freshly pressed dress. The boy wore dress pants that looked like they were brand new. They both smelled of strong soap, a smell that competed with the animal smell of anger that dominated the air around them. The boy was swinging his feet around beneath his chair, and his apparently new shoes, which were polished to a bright shine, became the focus of all eyes for a brief moment until he noticed and stopped to sit dead still.

Helen pulled Sis by the hand and stepped closer. The red high heels clicked sharply against the hard floor. She pointed to the chair that was one down from the boy.

"Sit down, Sis," she said.

The girl sat down uncertainly.

Then Helen sat down next to the boy, her eyes scanning the group of parents across from them for any sign of change. The mother let go of the boy's hand and put her left arm around his shoulder, pulling him closer to her. This caused him to sit in an awkward slanted position that emphasized his discomfort.

Helen spoke without taking her eyes off the crowd of stone faces, hanging above them like fierce gargoyles attached to invisible wires.

"I'm Helen Wasilec, Mrs. Jefferson," she said. "Your boy is entering my daughter's class today."

"He is entering today," the woman said, her body straightened even more, as if she was turning her courage up another level. Her unsteady voice betrayed her, but her determination was clear. "Don't nobody try to change my mind," she said to Helen, loud enough for the assembled parents to hear.

Helen extended her right hand to the woman whose eyes brimmed with a timeworn distrust. "I'm not here to change your mind," Helen said. "I'm here to welcome you."

The negro mother stared at the small, freckled hand.

"Please, Mrs. Jefferson. Don't let them see you're afraid. It will encourage them."

Mrs. Jefferson hesitated, then raised her right hand to Helen's and shook it.

Everyone's eyes were on the unlikely foursome; and the muffled voices kept up the rhythm of statement, agreement, statement, agreement.

"Good, Mrs. Jefferson. Now let your boy go with my daughter to his class," Helen said. She meant to guide but appeared to command.

The other mother moved back into the straight chair, pulling her son with her, making his already stretched torso look
contorted and strange. "I'm not letting my Leonard out of my
sight!"

As her voice rose slightly, the crowd's voices seemed to rise
also, and Helen could hear some of what they were saying.

"I'll pull my kids out too."

"They won't have any kids to teach."

"Sure, we'll start our own school."

How foolish can these people get? Helen thought. *Everyone knows Horace Mann is one of the best grade schools in
Alton.*

The crowd became quiet for a moment. Then a man's
voice sounded clearly above the crowd, but there was no face
connected with the words.

"I've half a mind to move." Other anonymous mothers and
fathers started stirring again, the anger rising up, thick and
smothering like summer air before a thunderstorm.

"That's not going to happen," another man near the back
of the crowd answered. "No coloreds are pushing us out of
our homes."

Helen spoke up this time. "You sound like idiots. All this
fuss over one small colored child!"

Another undistinguished looking parent in the front row
answered, "Sure, it's one now, but once you let coloreds in,
it'll go downhill," he said, shaking his head at Helen, then
turning to the crowd, "Right?"

"Damned right, Herman!" A father's voice spoke out.

"It's happened before. Look at Roosevelt school." A mother
said. "All those fights they have now."

"What fights?" Helen asked. *I don't want Sis to be around
kids starting fights*, she thought.

"There was a big one after the football game two weeks ago," another voice said.

"Alton teams always fight with the Granite City teams," Helen said, regaining her focus.

"With knives?" a voice asked.

The crowd took up the words, and they floated above their heads, just loud enough to make out.

"No fights."

"*No* knives."

"We've got to stop this now."

"Knives!"

"The little kids could get hurt, knives or not."

Helen knew she had to do something, but she was not as sure as she had been. She didn't want knives or weapons of any kind at Sis's school.

"Roosevelt isn't a bad school," she said. "My sister Philomena teaches there. She hasn't said anything about knives."

"After the game."

"It was in the paper."

"For the love of Mike," she yelled. "We don't have football games at Horace Mann." Helen realized how desperate and ridiculous this sounded.

A disheveled looking woman in a dingy house dress offered her opinion. "Look how rundown that school's getting."

Her husband angrily backed her up. "The niggers have ruined it."

Sis tugged at Helen's dress. "Mr. Turner said that bad word."

Helen didn't like the term, or the sound of Turner's voice. She tried to act as if she had not heard it. "The school board doesn't put any money into repairs now because it's a colored school. That's why it's rundown," Helen said, her eyes bright with anger. "I'll say it again, you're all damned fools to be so upset over one small boy." She turned and pointed to Leonard, whose eyes were downcast, still looking at his shoes.

"It will be better if you let him go." Helen said to Mrs. Jefferson, switching tactics from command to persuasion. "It's you they're afraid of, I promise you they won't hurt him." Mrs. Jefferson still refused.

"These people are my neighbors," Helen spoke, looking back into the crowd who watched attentively, but did not move any closer or farther away. For all their angry expressions, Helen thought they looked more frightened than dangerous, like a herd of sheep, scared by loud barking and nipping at their heels. "I know all these people, and they are not going to hurt a little boy!"

"You don't think they hurts little boys in this town," the woman said, contempt filling out her words.

"Not today, not while I'm around they don't," Helen replied, all the uncertainty gone from her voice and the strength of will that always served her well coming through, leaving no doubt that she believed she could back this up.

"Sis, take Leonard with you and go to your classroom," Helen commanded. "Mrs. Mussman is waiting."

Sis started to get up, reaching for the little boy's hand.

"No." Mrs. Jefferson's voice was just as commanding as Helen's now.

Leonard sat rigid, except for his eyes which turned to his mother for guidance. "I'm not letting him out of my sight."

The crowd was moving in closer again and a voice that sounded like Johnny Carpenter's said, "Are we going to let this happen?"

A couple of voices answered, "No way," but no one stepped forward to challenge Helen face to face.

For a minute or two Helen Wasilec felt beaten, all this craziness. It wasn't like the family was moving into the neighborhood. The kids would never even see the boy, except at school. She didn't like the unfamiliar feeling she was having. She could always work problems out in groups. Maybe not always with Joe Sr, but with other people, there was always a way. Only a few seconds had passed before Helen thought of what to do and spoke to the boy's mother again.

"Mrs. Jefferson, did you have a voter registration coffee during the last election?" Helen asked.

"How do you know that?"

"I set it up, remember. I was at your house."

The woman looked at Helen more closely, her face registering disbelief.

"I called and asked you to do it." Helen had paid Mrs. Jefferson $7.50 because she got eleven women besides herself to come, and five of them had decided to register. It was one dollar per voter, and $2.50 for having the party. "I remember your house, because it was the biggest turnout we had."

Mrs. Jefferson's face brightened with recognition. She had used the money to buy an extra present for the boy that Christmas and a bigger tree than usual.

The recognition on Mrs. Jefferson's part was Helen's opening. She moved toward an empty chair, talking to her daughter. "Sis, stand up and fold your chair."

The girl got up and followed her mother's lead.

"Come on, Mrs. Jefferson. We'll take these chairs, and you and I will sit outside our children's classroom as long as you want."

Mrs. Jefferson was the one who did not know what to do now. Helen reached out her hand to Leonard, holding the folded chair under her other arm.

"Come on, Leonard. No one's going to hurt you."

The young boy looked at his mother to see if he should go.

Helen saw Mrs. Jefferson's look of doubt mixed with acceptance. *She must think I'm a crazy woman in my red, white, and blue outfit, like the 4th of July,* Helen thought. *So, sure, I can fend off these people who clearly hate coloreds, even women and children.* Helen was learning that hatred born of fear was as strong as hatred born of experience.

Mrs. Jefferson stood up quickly. "I'll take him myself, thank you!" she said, taking Leonard's hand back into her own and motioning for him to stand.

"All right, that's better," Helen said, a note of cheer sounding in her voice. She turned to her daughter and nodded in the direction of the classrooms. "Go on, Sis. We'll follow you."

For a moment it looked as if the group of parents that were watching all of this, grumbling threats under their voices, were going to block the children's way.

Helen walked a little closer to Sis and the boy and glared at the protestors. "Get out of our way."

No one moved.

"Now!"

People started shuffling around, muttering. "We gonna let her get away with this?"

"Don't seem right? I always thought you could depend on Helen."

"I'll be damned if I ever vote with the Democrats again."

As the grumbling died down, the crowd began to part, leaving a narrow path in the middle for the two mothers and children to pass.

Helen's chest moved slightly downward as she released her breath in an unexpected sigh. She had not been as sure as she sounded. She gave Sis another nudge, pointing down the hall.

When the foursome moved away from the door, the principal, who had been observing the scene from inside the haven of his glass walled outer office, stepped in behind them. Some of the parents, obviously relieved, turned to leave, while others headed down the hall with what now looked like a planned procession.

When they got to the second-grade classroom, a smiling Mrs. Mussman welcomed the children by giving both of them a hug. All the other students in the class were wiggling around in their seats, trying to get a look at the new boy. Some frowned when they saw him, a natural response to their parents' teachings. Some smiled and giggled, pointing their fingers at him the way they did at animals in the zoo.

Still, none of the students got up from their desks, each one knowing that Mrs. Mussman would have a strong punishment for such behavior. The mid-morning sunlight shone in, illuminating the bright colored pictures on the walls, signed in every color of the rainbow—Mary Jones, Belinda Burk, Johnny Wells.

Sis had just enough time to show Leonard hers, the one with a pony in it, before Mrs. Mussman asked them to sit down at their desks. The teacher directed Leonard to a desk placed judiciously close to hers in the front of the room, and in direct contradiction to her normal habit, the teacher left her classroom door open.

Darlita Jefferson and Helen Wasilec sat in the hall outside Mrs. Mussman's open classroom door for three full weeks before the last dissenting parents decided to give up the standoff, and Mrs. Jefferson was convinced that Leonard was safe.

There was some vandalism at the school. A brick thrown through the front window of the school, black paint sloshed onto the sidewalk, and the words, "Coloreds go away," was painted on the steel front doors.

Only one newspaper article was written about the mothers, but it had a picture of them sitting together, showing Helen

Wasilec doing embroidery while Mrs. Jefferson mended. They hardly talked. Sis and Leonard became friends, but their mothers were never more than polite acquaintances. Two women who did no more or less than what they felt they had to do.

Sis taught Leonard to play some schoolyard games, though none of the other kids wanted to play with them which made it difficult. Leonard taught her to shoot a basket. Playing horse was a good game for two. Sis's best friends, June and Carole, still played with her after school and on weekends, but they never played with her and Leonard.

After the mothers' vigil ended, Helen Wasilec started letting Sis's chow dog follow Sis to school in the morning, a practice which had been stopped the year before because the dog threatened to bite a child who playfully slapped Sis on the back. At noon the dog went to meet Sis, and after lunch, he walked her back. When school was out, the dog was always outside the school door waiting for Sis, ready to make sure she got home safely. No one would dare touch Sis Wasilec with the chow around.

Joe Wasilec also had a chain link fence built around their house, but their neighbors were more subtle than to attack their homestead and strangers didn't know where they lived. The phone rang much less often for several months.

Sis asked her mother directly, stringing a lot of questions and thoughts together the way children do. "People don't like Leonard because he's colored? Why, Mom?"

"I don't think they really don't like Leonard," Helen answered. "They just don't understand him because he's different."

"You said he's not different inside? You said to respect everyone, no matter how different they are, what they look like, how smart they are."

"That was when you said you didn't like Nelson Burch because he was ugly and dumb. Those aren't nice thoughts."

"Not liking Leonard isn't nice either. I wish someone else liked Leonard, too. Their mothers should tell them what you told me."

No one in the family tried to explain any of this to Sis or talked about the incident and its ramifications in front of her. Winter came, and recesses ceased until spring.

By spring, Sis didn't seem to care that, with the exception of Lindell Gray, who lived in a little house down past the woods near the railroad tracks, she was the only one who talked with Leonard much, or sat by him at the lunchroom, or played with him in the gym. When Mrs. Kolbert invited the whole class to Carole's birthday party, all of the girls and most of the boys were there, but Leonard was not.

"Mrs. Kolbert, is Leonard coming?" Sis asked.

"No, dear, he lives so far away." Mrs. Kolbert smiled a white lie smile. "I didn't think his mom would want to bring him back on a Saturday."

When she got home, Sis ran to her mother, who was fixing a pork roast with mashed potatoes and gravy, creamed corn, and wilted lettuce salad for Saturday night dinner. "Mom, Leonard wasn't at the party."

"I'm not surprised."

"I asked Carole's mom why he wasn't there, and she said he lived too far away to come back over here on Saturday."

Helen smiled the same smile Mrs. Kolbert had. "She's probably right."

"I think that's silly," Sis shook her head. "When my birthday comes, Dad will go pick Leonard up, won't he?"

Helen Wasilec had not learned to drive.

"Of course not," Helen said.

"Why not?"

"Because Mrs. Kolbert is right about it being too far, and 1 don't think Leonard would be comfortable at your party anyway."

"I want Leonard at my party, Mama. It's wrong to invite everyone else and not invite him."

Helen saw the confusion and defiance on Sis's face, the sense of betrayal, and wondered if her daughter would ever listen to her again.

"I'm going to invite him Monday, so he knows I want him to come."

"You'll do no such thing, Sis Wasilec," Helen said. "And if you keep this up, you're going to bed immediately after supper."

"I don't understand." Sis was beginning to cry. "Why can't Leonard come to my party?"

"For god's sake, Sis," Helen said. "He's colored."

A Special Family Sunday
Alton, IL — circa 1951

The first inkling that anything was going to change was a late spring Sunday night just before Sis's bedtime. Joe Sr. and she finished listening to their radio programs together, Sis on his lap in the sunroom rocking chair in front of the old console radio handed down from Grandma Wasilec when all her sons got together and bought her a new one. After the "Lone Ranger" signed off, Joe moved into the living room.

Helen was so tired that she barely felt her ten-year-old daughter tugging on her wet apron like a toddler does, trying to get her attention. Even though most of Helen's clothes were house dresses, she always tried to keep them nice by wearing aprons.

Sis's voice finally penetrated Helen's Sunday night haze. "Mama," Sis said, "I've got something to tell you."

Helen looked into her daughter's face and saw excitement but ignored it. "Are you ready for bed?"

"No."

"Well, don't you think you'd better get ready? It's almost a half-hour past time."

"Mom, this is important."

"You have school in the morning."

"I need to tell you what Dad said. He asked me how I'd like to have a little brother."

"What?"

"Dad asked me if I'd like to have a little brother," Sis paused. "I told him I'd rather have a sister!"

"Sis, when are you going to stop pestering about this?"

"Honest, Dad asked *me*. And I finally said 'okay.' If I can't have a little sister, a brother will do."

"Forget it. It's not going to happen."

"Why not?"

Helen took off the wet apron, put her arm around Sis, and said, "Let's get you to bed."

"Is it my fault, Mama?"

"What?"

"Is it my fault you don't want another baby?"

"No, of course, not. Where'd you get that idea?"

"Everybody knows I was such a big baby that you got sick."

"Where did you hear that?"

"From Aunt Phil. She said I was too big a baby, and you got diabetes."

"You were a big baby. Remember I told you I was worried that I didn't have booties to take you home from the hospital. One of the nuns laughed and said, 'You should just put shoes on her and let her walk home.'"

Sis liked that story, and it usually gave them both a chuckle. Not this night.

"You have to believe me, Sis. No one is to blame. Especially not you!"

Of course, the doctor had blamed the baby. She was "too big," he said. "Over eleven pounds. Damaged your system . . . that's why you have diabetes." Apparently, Helen's older sister, Philomena, blamed Sis, too.

"Mama, I want a little sister so bad."

"Your friend Junie is almost like a sister."

"It's not the same."

"You get what you get." Helen repeated what she herself was told too many times to count. "You have to be happy with it."

Helen didn't get a chance to talk to Joe Sr. that night, or the next morning. She would look back and regret that.

• • •

The Sunday night Benny came into their lives was unremarkable except for his arrival and the fact that Joe Sr. had left early in the morning, as he always did, but even though he knew Helen was making Joe's favorite short ribs with mashed potatoes and gravy, sauteed cabbage, and creamed baby onions, he didn't come home for dinner. Per their agreement, he could do whatever his heart desired Sunday morning and afternoon, but he was never to miss their family Sunday dinner. Helen had even made a coconut cream pie, another of his favorites. The meringue stood three inches high.

Joe Sr. knew Helen's diabetes required her to stick to a rigid schedule for meals. The family ate at 5:00 PM, as usual, Joe or no Joe.

Fortunately, neither of Helen's older sisters asked her to explain Joe's absence. They were generally happier when he wasn't around. He cursed too much for her oldest sister, Philomena, whom everyone called Aunt Phil. And Laura Mae, Aunt Boots to the family, invariably got into arguments with Joe Sr. over union conflicts at Owens Illinois Glass Works. She was Congress of Industrial Organizations (CIO), he was American Federation of Labor (AFL).

If they had asked, Helen would have told them a white lie, said she hadn't expected him, that she knew he'd be eating out, and she had made that special Sunday night dinner "just for us."

By the time Helen began to do dishes, she had convinced herself that Joe would have been home, had meant to be home, but was unavoidably delayed, not by one of his women, but perhaps by a terrible traffic accident . . . he might even be hurt . . . dead . . . killed, right on the spot.

Sis's dog was the first one to hear Joe's Buick, a hard-topped convertible, come up the driveway. He barked a jubilant welcome. Sis was at the back door to greet her dad before Helen could put down the pan she was scrubbing and wipe the suds off her hands. Sis was the first to see the boy. She saw him through the screen door.

He was a small boy, scrawny for a six-year-old. Joe Sr. lifted him onto the square wooden stoop off the back door and handed him a weekend-sized suitcase.

He was dressed in a little boy's grey dress suit, with a starched white shirt and a black bow tie. His shoes were shined to perfection, clearly for a special occasion, not 8:30 PM on a Sunday night.

Sis just stood there as Joe Sr. opened the screen door and pushed Ben into the mudroom. Her eyes followed her father, then the boy, and then looked questioningly at Helen.

When Helen's hands were finally dry, she moved toward them, wondering who this little fellow was and why Joe had brought him home with the obvious intention of his staying a while. The conversation with Sis several weeks earlier lay hidden in the back of her mind.

"Helen, this is your new son, Ben," Joe said in his gruff voice. Then he turned to Sis, and said, "This is your new little brother. He likes to be called Benny."

The man was as casual as if he were handing Helen a sack of groceries. Although it was a warm night, the boy was shivering. "Take care of him," Joe said. "I need to get the rest of his things."

Lot's wife could have moved to the boy faster than Helen did. She heard herself say, "Sis, would you take Benny into the living room and rock him while I talk to your Dad?"

For once, Sis did what she was told without the slightest hesitation or question.

Sis took Benny's hand, put her arm around his thin shoulders and walked him to the ladder-backed rocker in the living room. Once in her lap in the rocker, he cuddled into the crook of her arm like a lost puppy does when picked up for the first time. Sis began rocking him, singing a song Helen sang to her when she was younger.

"Hush, little boy, don't you cry. Mommy's going to sing you a lullaby . . . buy you a mockingbird . . ."

From where Sis and Benny were, Sis could see straight through to the kitchen. Her Mom hadn't moved from the exact spot where she had been earlier, but her dad came into the living room with another small suitcase and a multi-colored afghan that looked like it had been crocheted with great love.

Without a word to his daughter or his wife, Joe Sr. unfolded the afghan and wrapped it gently around Benny who had fallen asleep in Sis's arms. Then he returned to Helen in the mudroom where she was staring out into the night.

Sis couldn't make out their words, but her mom and dad were really angry, both of their faces making grimaces and getting redder than her mom's did when she had her hands in the scalding dish water. And their voices kept getting louder and louder.

Although Aunt Phil had gone sound asleep early, full of short ribs and coconut pie, Aunt Boots was still awake. She came downstairs to see what was causing such a ruckus. She did this a lot when she heard fights because she was always afraid Joe would hurt Helen someday.

When Aunt Boots saw Benny asleep, curled up in her niece's arms with his bur haircut and small face showing above the afghan, she stood there looking at him, staring at his face.

Then she said, "Come on Sis, let's get this little guy to bed."

"Where can we put him?" Sis asked.

"How about your bed, then when he wakes up your mom and dad will be in the bed right beside him.

"In the upper bunk?"

"No, the lower bunk, your bed!"

"But where will I sleep? I can't sleep in the upper bunk. I sleepwalk."

"How about coming upstairs and sleeping with me? I'll close the child's gate at the top of the stairs. The one I use when my grandkids are visiting."

"But what about Mom? Who'll tell her where I am?"

"I think she'll figure it out," Boots said. "Come on now, let's look in these suitcases and see if this little guy has some pajamas to sleep in."

Boots helped Sis take him into the big bedroom, take off his suit down to his undershirt and briefs, put on his PJs, and tuck him into Sis's bed.

Sis thought about how scared he must have been when her dad picked him up. Someone packed the two suitcases with everything he owned. You sure could not have gotten all her things in them. You would have needed a trunk.

After he was sound asleep again with a beat-up brown teddy bear that they found in one of the suitcases, Sis started to say something to Aunt Boots, but Boots raised her finger to her lips in the universal "shhhh!" gesture and pointed up the stairs.

Once Sis and Boots were upstairs getting ready for bed themselves, Sis asked her aunt the big question. "Where do you think Dad got him?"

"God knows!" Boots said, "I surely don't have the faintest."

"But he has to be somebody's little boy."

"Never you mind now. Get to sleep. You've got school in the morning."

School, Sis thought. Was she going to have to go to school with a new brother at home?

Looking back, she wondered how she fell asleep that night. Mom and Dad were still "talking" in the kitchen. Aunt Boots had gone to the top of the steps, just out of sight, to listen.

Mom and Dad's voices were loud enough Sis could hear a few words herself. The sound came up through the gravity driven heat vent. She may have dreamed this because it seemed to come a long time after she got to sleep. Her mom was yelling, "Why?"

"Why didn't you tell me?"

"Would you have said 'yes?'"

"No, of course not!"

"That's why!"

Then Joe shouted, "I'm not going to stay here if you're hysterical," and slammed the back door so hard it shook the frame. "If you want me, I'll be at Mom's."

Helen finished the dishes, wandered around the backyard awhile, let the dog in, and locked the back doors. In the big bedroom, she found the boy sound asleep in Sis's bed, the covers pulled up over his head. He was in a deep sleep; and she wondered how he could sleep so soundly in a strange place and bed.

Next, she checked on her mother. Boots had put Grandma Hecht to bed. The anger that caused Helen to yell at Joe Sr.

had passed. She felt numb one minute and bewildered the next, bereft.

Helen sat on the second step of the stairs, just outside her mother's door, petting the dog and crying. That's where Boots found her. Boots had waited for Sis to fall asleep before she came back down to check on her younger sister.

Boots seldom got credit for her nurturing abilities because Helen was the "domestic queen" of the house. That night, Boots put her arms around Helen, stroked her hair and back, and for that moment in time, Helen did not cringe at being touched.

Helen finally stopped crying long enough to ask the obvious question. "Do you think he's Joe's?"

Boots laughed. "I took a good look at him earlier," she said. "That boy doesn't have one drop of Wasilec blood."

The next morning at breakfast, after Helen fed Sis, helped the boy find some casual clothes, and made him wash his face and hands, she finally got a good look at Ben. The boy had an olive complexion, dark brown eyes, and a minutely hooked nose. Helen had to admit he was cute. Also sweet and polite, though very shy. "Not a drop of Wasilec blood," Boots had said, and Helen saw that she was right.

When Helen offered Ben another egg and some more toast, he asked, "Does it cost extra?"

"No, honey, it doesn't cost anything," Helen said. Then touching the top of his head with a soft pat, she added, "You don't have to worry about how much it costs now. You're home."

A physical shock ran through Sis's body. She realized Benny was really staying.

Benny's question to Helen about the egg's cost came from his having been on the road most of his life—living on trains, in motels, and in hotel rooms with his father, who was a gambling pal of Joe Sr.

• • •

Gambling was legal in Illinois when Sis was growing up in the 1940s and early 1950s. Joe Sr. made extra money at a place called Nick's just outside the city limits of Alton, in East Alton. He was the house man, a person who gambled with the owner's money and got a percentage cut of everything he won.

He was pretty good, too. The spring after Benny arrived, Helen had to go to Deaconess Hospital in Boston. One night Joe Sr. came home with all the money he had won. Nick let him keep it all to help with the trip.

What a night that was! Joe Sr. woke everyone up to count the money. It came to three hundred fifty dollars and seventy-six cents. Sis never forgot sitting around that big old kitchen table counting change and dollar bills. Each person made stacks of ten dollars except Benny. He was counting pennies into stacks of ten. Then they put them all together. It took about an hour. Joe Sr. made all that money in one night.

• • •

Sis's father and Benny's father met in their poker playing circles and became good friends. When Big Ben, after a night of hard playing and drinking, crashed his Cadillac into a telephone pole, killing Benny's young mother immediately, he was taken to Barnes Hospital in St. Louis where he asked for his first wife, Doreen, and his friend Joe Wasilec.

The dying man's last wish was for Joe Sr. to adopt and raise little Ben. It never occurred to Joe to refuse. Benny's father died with the comfort of knowing that his son would grow up in a family. Doreen always said she knew that was best, but Helen thought—and Aunt Boots often said—Doreen would have loved to raise him herself.

After she was older, Sis wondered how her mom survived all this. The new child, the new people in their lives, some with somewhat unsavory personas, she didn't think much about it in those days. Later she realized how hard it must have been for her mom. Helen just carried on.

To add to the bizarre nature of the whole situation, Joe Sr. and Doreen inserted an element of danger into it, not just for Benny, but for everyone in the family.

"Big Benny's family is Jewish," Joe Sr. said. "They sure wouldn't want his son to go to a Catholic family. We knew they wouldn't want the boy though. They might put him in a Jewish Children's Home."

"Could they do that?" Helen asked.

"I couldn't let them," Doreen said. "That's why I kidnapped him."

"Kidnapped!" Helen said.

"They didn't even come to the hospital," Doreen said. "So, as soon as Big Ben died, I took Benny and went to Texas for several months. I heard through the grapevine that the FBI was after me. Didn't come back 'til I was sure they were off my track."

Helen told Sis that, according to Joe Sr., when Doreen felt it was safe, she returned to the St. Louis area with Benny, who then stayed with another family until Joe could be reached.

Joe had close ties with this other family, apparently through his connection to the wife. With only a tenth of the resentment Helen used to feel, she wondered if Joe had slept with the wife. She decided that was a given. Though she never really thought he had slept with Doreen.

Did Helen believe this convoluted story, including that the FBI was looking for the boy? It was as good as any she herself could have made up. Helen was accomplished at making up "white lies" to excuse Joe's behavior.

Did Sis believe this story? Of course. Her dad said it was true and her mom said it was true. Ten-year-olds believe their parents.

Helen quoted this tale to everyone in the family, including Aunt Phil, Aunt Boots, Sis's older brother, Joe Jr., Grandma Hecht, Grandma Wasilec, all the brothers of Joe Sr. and their wives, and all of Helen's friends.

Did they believe it? Helen never questioned that.

After Sis was a few years older, she noticed how much Benny looked like Aunt Boots's son, her cousin Dan. She asked her mom if Benny was really Dan's son.

"Why in the world did you think that?" Helen asked.

"Because Benny looks just like Dan. Don't you see it?"

"No, I don't. And if your Aunt Boots ever heard that you thought such a thing," Helen said, "she'd probably give you a fanny tanning."

Because of the "kidnapping" issue, Joe Sr. was especially conscious that Benny could be taken away. Everyone in the family was instructed that he was never to be out of sight. Not that Joe Sr. was around to watch out for the boy, but he took great care to impress upon everyone else how important this was.

Helen added emphasis to this with Sis. Helen told Sis again and again that she and Benny were never to talk to strangers or let strangers near Ben. Helen did not tell her that the FBI was looking for him. What did Sis know about the FBI?

Sis's dog was an Ozark hills cur, a breed that is now recognized by some hunting dog organizations, but was as far as everyone knew then, a Heinz dog, 57 varieties. He had a pink tongue variegated with purple—which showed he was part Chow—and a protective nature towards the whole family, but especially Sis. For all the times when Benny was out playing or going to and from school or walking to a friend's, Sis was his guardian, and thus, he also was under Ozark's protection.

There never were any strange cars watching the house or following the family, even when "Aunt" Doreen, a title

Doreen readily accepted, visited Alton or the family went to see her in St. Louis. Not that Helen expected any. Helen was sure that the whole FBI thing was a fabrication of Joe's to keep her mind off the fact that he had "dropped" a son in her lap on an ordinary Sunday night.

No matter how Helen felt about Joe's involvement with Benny, or Doreen, or Big Benny, she could not let that affect how she felt about her youngest child.

And Sis's heart would have been irreparably broken if they had lost Benny. He was her little brother.

The day Helen realized how much she loved Benny, despite the way he came to her, was the day she and Joe adopted him. Because Helen was active in local politics, helping to elect more than one circuit court judge, she was able to convince one of them to rush Benny's adoption through. The legal proceedings took place in Judge Amerfelt's private chambers. The judge, the court clerk, Joe, Doreen, who was an important witness, Sis, Benny, and Helen were the only people present.

After the testimony the judge asked Benny to step forward. "Benny, do you want to be legally adopted into the Joseph and Helen Wasilec family?" Ben's response surprised everyone.

"No, sir, not unless . . ." Benny said.

Everyone was so upset, whispering back and forth to each other, that the judge had to ask for quiet so that he could hear the last of what Benny had said.

"Young man, you have surprised us. We thought you wanted to be a Wasilec."

"I love my new mom and dad," he said. "I just don't want to be adopted unless they can adopt Sissy, too, so no one will ever take her away."

Not one witness could keep from smiling except the judge, who looked down from his lofty seat and with his most serious voice said, "I promise you that if you are adopted, no one will ever take either you or Sissy away."

"Okay," Ben said. "I want to be adopted."

• • •

After the adoption, Helen's doubts about part or all of what Joe and Doreen had told her of Benny's birth, the accident, his mother's death, and finally, Big Ben's death, became stronger. Doreen's testimony during the adoption procedure was appreciably different from the original story. Doreen swore under oath that she was married to Big Ben at the time of his death, as well as vowing that Benny's mother had died shortly after childbirth from an unspecified disease. Thus, as Big Ben's lawful wife, Doreen could relinquish parental rights for Benny to Joe and his wife.

As troubling as this could have been, Helen didn't dwell on it. She put Benny's mother's identity out of her mind as she did many other inconvenient or unpleasant facts and thoughts.

Helen's illness grew worse and Joe Sr. grew further away from the family. The one thing that Helen insisted on was Family Sundays.

Helen told Joe, "I don't care what we do," which she regretted saying when he took the family to meet a young stripper-friend of his "but you are going to spend Sunday with your family."

Thus, if Aunt Doreen was not visiting the Wasilecs, they went to St. Louis to visit "Aunt" Doreen. She was always happy to share trips to Shaw's Botanical Gardens, the St. Louis Zoo, the Jewel Box, or the riverfront, and then treat the Wasilecs to dinner at the Golden Fried Chicken where Helen enjoyed the homemade chicken soup that fit right in to her diabetic diet or to one of the great St. Louis barbeque joints where the smoky sweet barbeque sauce did not fit into her diet plan. Helen enjoyed the ribs anyway. Doreen was happy wherever she was if Ben was there.

Aunt Doreen became just another member of the big, conjoined family, often spending weekends with them at their home, enjoying the long front porch and Helen's flower gardens as much as the Wasilecs enjoyed the sights of St. Louis.

One spring weekend, shortly after Joe and Helen adopted Benny, they all went on a day trip to visit Doreen's family. Helen asked Laura Mae along.

"It's a reunion, of sorts," Aunt Doreen said.

When they got there, Helen and Boots both noticed how much Doreen's sister, Inez, who was twenty years younger with toddlers of her own, was taken with Ben.

The younger woman spent the whole afternoon playing with Ben—talking to him, reading him books, and taking at least two rolls of Polaroid film. Helen took a lot of pictures with her Brownie camera that day, too. There were several times when Doreen's younger sister, Inez, asked them to take a picture of her with Benny and her two children. Or her and Doreen and Benny. Or her and her husband with Benny and the girls. Everyone truly enjoyed the day.

The Wasilecs never visited Doreen's younger sister again. Sometimes, Helen felt a palpable sorrow about that for Benny. For as much as their whole family loved him, from Helen, to Joe Sr., to Joe Jr., to Philomena, to Laura Mae and her kids, and especially, to Sis, Helen always thought he looked like he really belonged in the pictures she took at Inez's that Family Sunday in May.

The "You Can Buy Anything Strip"
St. Louis, MO — 1950s

Every time Helen Wasilec crossed the mile-long Clark Bridge over the Mississippi River and the shorter Lewis Bridge over the Missouri River, whether she was going for a Sunday drive with Joe Sr. at the wheel of his flashy, boat-sized Buick with Sis and Benny in the back, to a doctor's appointment, on a shopping trip, or to see the Christmas decorations in the big department store windows in downtown St. Louis, she wondered if it was her last. Especially when the trip was to see the city all decked out for Christmas with Santa Clauses ringing bells on every corner, the windows full of mechanical elves, reindeer, and happy mechanical children opening presents by gas-fired hearths, Helen knew she was living on borrowed time.

The specialists at Deaconess Hospital in Boston managed to save her toes in 1950, but they said she would be lucky if she lived another ten years. Of course, she didn't really believe that. With Frank Jr. grown and away from home, Helen asked God to let her live until all of her children were settled and safe, and God never let Helen down on the big things.

I want to live until Benny is out of high school; I want to see him graduate, Helen thought, as she loosened the dirt around the irises. *I want to see Sis settled. I have to live five years longer than they said. Nineteen sixty-four.*

Helen felt this trip would be even more special than Christmas. She looked at her daughter, Sis, sitting next to her at the window, watching the Mississippi River swirling below, and knew that Sis was thinking about all the places the river went, wondering if she would ever see them. Helen knew this because she and her sisters had done the same when they were sixteen, when they took the interurban railroad from Grafton to Alton and across the Mississippi to St. Louis.

Sis was old enough to drive and often drove Helen to her appointments with the diabetes specialist in Clayton, but that was suburban St. Louis. Helen wasn't quite comfortable with the prospect of Sis driving in downtown St. Louis traffic. Besides, Helen enjoyed taking the Brown Bus, it gave her quiet time to plan, and the steady, bumpy progress of the bus was relaxing, not like when Joe Sr. drove the family to St. Louis on Sundays for dinner. On the trip home, Joe Sr. would drive carelessly just to upset Helen, causing a row that would, at least in his thinking, justify his going off to see his current girlfriend that evening.

Helen remembered the last such argument. Sis was on the phone, standing with one shapely leg up on a chair, her elbow resting on the top so that she could lean into the earpiece, her hip swung out toward the picture window, its lace curtain open to let in the afternoon sun. Helen smiled, thinking, *Sis reminds me of myself at her age.*

"Mom, can I go with Billy to the movies tomorrow afternoon?"

"Billy Burton?"

"Moooom!"

"Billy who then?" Helen called from the small kitchen adjoining the hunter green living and dining room combination.

"Billy Minnelli, remember? I met him last week at Sara's church hayride."

"Billy Minnelli," Joe shouted from his seat at the end of the couch, facing the twenty-one-inch TV, his cigar falling from his mouth onto the cushion beside him. "No daughter of mine is going out with that Dago Minnelli's son."

"Joe, you know how I hate you to use words like that, what if someone called you a Polack."

"I am a Polack, a dumb one too; I married you, didn't I?"

Helen winced but went on, "What can it hurt to let her go to the movies with the boy?"

Helen turned to Sis who was covering the speaker end of the phone so Billy Minnelli couldn't hear the family discussion. "Were you going to the Uptown Theater?"

"Yes, Billy doesn't have a car. We're going to walk."

"He's old enough to have a car, and he's old enough to know what the back seat's for." Joe jumped up from his heavily worn place on the couch and grabbed the phone from Sis's hand. "No! She can't go! Don't call here again!"

"Dad, how could you?" Sis said, her face turning bright red and her eyes entreating him.

"Where did you say you met him?"

"At Sara's church hayride. We sat next to each other."

By now, Helen was standing beside Sis to protect her from Joe's rage, a symptom of Joe's temperament, but also of his knowledge that Sis was the most important thing in the world to his wife. He never hit Helen, Sis, or Benny, but Joe Jr. had gotten his share of beatings when he was still at home. Joe grabbed Helen by the arm and half-dragged, half-pushed her into the small alcove in the kitchen that housed the sink and the kitchen cabinets.

"How many times am I going to have to tell you Sis is not to go to that bible thumper's church? These kids are going to be Catholic no matter what kind of half-cocked religions their friends have."

Just go, Joe, Helen thought. *It's almost Saturday night. You have your excuse now, just go.*

"Sis, get in here." Joe called to his daughter whose face showed all the signs of the hatred these brawls were fostering. "You didn't do anything you shouldn't with that Minnelli boy, did you?"

"No, Dad!"

"Did he touch you?"

"What do you mean?"

Helen wanted to scream, but she knew it was best to let him rant.

"Did he touch you anywhere?"

"We held hands," Sis was getting scared. "That's all."

"Did he kiss you?"

"Dad, it was a church thing."

"So, you would have let him kiss you, but it was a church thing, you slut!"

For a minute Helen thought he would slap Sis, but he didn't, he just turned away slowly. "Slut! Whore! You'll be pregnant before you're out of high school. Just like your mother."

Helen saw the expression on Sis's face. There was nothing she could do. The secret was out, and the pain of that was probably even worse than the pain a smack up the side of the face would have been. She started back toward her child, to take her in her arms, but Joe was calling her into the bedroom. There would be more hollering while he changed clothes to go out, some orders about what Sis could and couldn't do, some orders for Helen to keep her busy ironing his work clothes or shining his shoes, anything he could think up to punish her, and then he'd be gone. The house would be peaceful for a while.

• • •

Both mother and daughter enjoyed their shopping trips to St. Louis. They spent many hours in Famous-Barr or Stix, Baer & Fuller. Sometimes they bought school clothes in the bargain basement. Helen particularly loved the bargain basement, bringing home numerous kitchen gadgets that were reduced fifty or sixty percent, or some new tool to work in her garden, a steal at seventy percent off. Generally, the trips were just an excuse to go to the city, window shop, and have a nice lunch out.

There were two shopping centers near St. Louis they could have gone to, but Helen Wasilec preferred walking around downtown. Sis was surprised when her mother suggested taking a streetcar to a different part of the city.

The steamy St. Louis heat wilted Sis's new blouse, but not her spirits. She tugged at her ponytail, trying to center it in the back, glad that her mother had insisted she put her hair up. The heat had frizzled Helen's darker blond hair into wispy ringlets around her face. Both women's blue eyes were bright with the excitement of an adventure. They took the Olive-Grand-Delmar streetcar, and Helen asked the woman driver to let her know when they got to DeBaliviere.

"Can you believe they'd have a woman driver in this traffic?" she said.

"They run on tracks, Mom!"

"Trains jump tracks. Why not streetcars?"

"Mom, you are so old-fashioned sometimes," Sis said, knowing this was an understatement, but not knowing what to pin her mother's attitudes on. "Women can do anything men can do. Look at Grandma Hecht and Aunt Phil who raised you and Aunt Boots after Grandpa was killed."

"That was because they had to. No woman has to drive a streetcar; she could be a teacher or a nurse," Helen said, pleased with her examples. "Women will be driving tractor trailer trucks next!"

When the driver called out their stop, Sis hoped they could get off at the side doors and avoid the inevitable, but Helen headed up the aisle to get off in the front. Hanging her slight body like a flag from the hand bar above her head, Helen leaned into the driver, "I just want to tell you how much I enjoyed the ride. I wasn't at all bothered that you are a woman."

The driver managed a "Thank you, Ma'am" without laughing and turned away. Sis, face red, eyes lowered, stepped off the bus as quickly as she could, thanking her luck that the driver was not black.

They headed toward the DeBaliviere Strip, a street noted for its diversity of shops, restaurants, music, and other amusements. Even in broad daylight, Sis saw that this was the kind of neighborhood Helen normally would avoid without a man along. She was surprised that her mother brought her here. There were some shops, an art theater, a Toddle House 24-hour breakfast spot, and a sleazy looking bar on their side of the street.

"Mom, are you sure this neighborhood is okay?"

"The Golden Fried Chicken is just a few blocks away from here on Delmar and there's a Velvet-Freeze ice cream shop down there," Helen said, pointing toward the corner of Lindell and DeBaliviere. "You know, they have great orange sherbet we sometimes get on Sunday." She smiled and kept pointing. "It's down there, near the entrance to Forest Park."

Sis looked in the direction her mother was pointing.

"See it?"

"Sort of."

"Would I take you anywhere that's not safe?"

Sis shook her head, no.

"Come on, Sissy, this will be fun. You can buy anything here."

They walked for a block, then Helen saw an oriental import shop. She stopped and peered into the window. "Look, is that jade?"

"What?"

"Those figurines." Helen peered closer, pressing her nose against the glass. "What does that little sign say?" She never wore her glasses in public, especially if Sis was there to read for her.

"'Ask to see special art collection—Chinese erotic figurines.' Just what we need for the curio case, Mom!"

"You're reading it wrong; it probably says exotic," Helen said.

"Yeah . . . like exotic dancers."

"What do you know about exotic dancers?"

Helen gave Sis one of her "I know you don't mean to upset me, but you are" looks and moved away from the window. She was intrigued by the VIP Travel agency sign in the window next door. Brilliantly colored pictures of green islands with snowcapped mountains and white sand beaches beckoned them to fly to Hawaii. "I'd like to go to Hawaii someday . . . Greece, maybe even Australia," Helen said.

Sis was briefly caught up in travel fantasies of her own, but Helen looked at her watch and interrupted them. "Almost noon. Look for Pat's Place," she said. "I thought we'd have lunch there."

"What about The Forum Cafeteria across the street from Famous-Barr?" Sis said.

"We always go there."

"It's your favorite place."

"I want to try something different."

"I was counting on bread pudding," Sis said.

"Bread pudding will make you fat."

"I'm solid, not fat," Sis said, repeating words her mother often said to her when she worried about her size. Sis, at sixteen, already had a grown woman's body, but Twiggy was the role model for teenagers in the late fifties.

"You will be fat if you don't watch it. You're built just like your dad. Thank God, you've got my legs and boobs though."

"Mom!"

"Yes, thank God."

"Mom, how many times do I have to ask you not to say things like that?"

"Like what?"

"You know, talking about my body parts."

"No one's around."

"Would it matter?" Sis said, gritting her teeth and glaring at her mother. They were still walking down the DeBaliviere Strip.

"Have I ever talked about your body parts in front of anyone else?"

"Yes."

"Who?"

"Aunt Boots."

"That doesn't count."

"Uncle Macon."

"Surely not!" Helen was sincerely shocked.

"Once."

"Okay, I'm sorry," Helen said. "Stop fussing and help me find Pat's Place."

They had gone almost the length of DeBaliviere. There were only two blocks left before Forest Park started.

"How'd you know about this Pat's Place, Mom?"

"I read about it in the weekend magazine in the *Post-Dispatch*. Then I remembered Grandpa Hecht used to talk about it."

Helen poured over the society and editorial pages of the *Post* every weekend, leaving the sports pages for Joe Sr. and Benny, although Benny was usually out shooting baskets. The entertainment pages were for Sis, who read every word. Helen had gotten Sis subscriptions to *Photoplay* and *Movie Times*, but Sis still liked the *Post-Dispatch* entertainment section because she always knew what plays and actors were coming to the American Theater, or in the summer to the Muny Opera. She dreamed of a time when a play she wrote would be performed at the American.

From time to time, Helen would point out that Grandpa Hecht knew this or that politician, but Sis never cared much about it. She did get excited when her mother said Grandpa actually met old Joe Kennedy somewhere along the way, but Grandpa died before John Kennedy made the nominating speech for Estes Kefauver for Vice-President in 1956 and became a household name, at least in the homes of Democrats.

• • •

Even Helen was not prepared for the time-honored luxury inside Pat's Place. Mother and daughter stood just inside the door, savoring every new sight—the heavy, wood-paneled interior, the bright brass bar rail, and the heavily ornamented mirror behind the bar. Why had her mother brought her here?

"I didn't expect it to be so elegant," Helen said.

"Me neither," Sis said, tucking a loose end of her white blouse into her form-fitted black pedal pushers. There was a long line of people waiting to be seated. Helen and Sis settled in to wait, looking at the pictures of celebrities on the wall beside them. There were sports and entertainment greats, and lots of prominent citizens of St. Louis.

Helen looked over the autographed photos and studio portraits, pointing some out to Sis. "Stan Musial . . . Sammy Gardner . . . Mel Tormé. Look at this. 'To Pat, Best Regards, Adlai Stevenson.' A Governor ate here!"

Sis looked at the photos, too, all different sizes and shots. Some had fancy wooden frames and others were simpler. She didn't recognize very many names. Then she saw it. An old shot in sepia tones, four men sitting in a booth, one standing beside it. It was signed, "To Pat and all my friends at the Place, Tennessee Williams."

"Mom, look, Tennessee Williams!"

"The country singer?"

"That's Tennessee Ernie Ford, Mom. No, the famous playwright. I know you know who I mean."

"You mean the famous degenerate who wrote all those plays that take place in the South." Helen gave Sis a disgusted look, but Sis ignored her.

"One took place in St. Louis."

"You and your writers. I wish you'd take an interest in really important people, men who make things happen in the world."

"Like Grandpa Hecht and his politician friends?" Sis said. "Turning a one street town into a one highway town isn't exactly earth shaking. Mom. I know, 'If Grandpa Hecht had lived longer, he would have put all of us into the history books.'"

"Yes, he would. He had a better chance than any of the other men in the family." Even though they were talking quietly, their voice tones were attracting stares. "I just wish you were interested in something useful, a practical way to use your mind and talent. Not everyone is given a really good brain like yours. You have to use it right. You aren't special in any other way."

Sis knew not to continue this conversation. Her mother had always made it clear that Sis was not special, which meant beautiful. Being smart wasn't the same as being beautiful. Smart got you nowhere. Men didn't like smart women. Helen never seemed to be able to think beyond Sis getting married. Even Helen's plans for Sis to go to college included a great catch.

"If you get a scholarship to St. Louis University or Washington University," Helen often said, "You'll meet boys that are studying to be doctors, lawyers, engineers. No laborers like your dad, for you."

"What good's that going to do me? You always say men don't like smart women. If I'm there on a scholarship, how am I going to meet a boy who wouldn't know?"

"You'll see. You can always make a man feel smarter than you."

"Maybe you can, but I can't. I don't even want to. I guess you're right though. The boys sure don't sit out in our yard and call 'Eula, Eula.' You know, like in the play, *The Long Hot Summer.*"

"What?"

"It's not important."

"As the line inched slowly forward, Sis looked up and crossed glances with a well-dressed, stockily built man talking to the maître d'. He had a thick shock of white hair that contrasted handsomely with his charcoal grey suit and tanned face. Sis thought he looked too young to have such white hair.

While he talked to the maître d', he occasionally glanced their way. Sis could hear a sentence or two.

"Come on, Jake. If Pat Jr. were here . . ."

"Sir, I'm not Pat Jr., and I don't have the authority."

"Now Jake." The man grinned and leaned in closer, in apparent jovial camaraderie. "Perhaps I could tell Pat about a few . . ." They weren't arguing, but there was an unpleasant tone to their banter.

Sis could not stop watching him, and he kept looking at her, and then Helen. After several minutes, he smiled broadly and moved toward them, his hands outstretched as if he were welcoming a close friend.

As he got nearer and started to speak to Helen, Sis noticed that he was older than she first thought, but still quite handsome. He reminded her of someone, but she couldn't think who.

"Excuse me, aren't you Helen Wasilec?" the man said.

Helen hadn't noticed him watching them, but she answered his question with a nod.

"I knew it was you, even though I haven't seen you since your father's funeral." The stranger clapped his fleshy red hands together, pleased with himself for recognizing her. "You haven't changed a bit since you were in your teens. I've heard that you are quite a politician in your own right since you've grown up and married."

The man's approach had startled Sis who stared wide-mouthed as her mother responded to the stranger with recognition.

"Mr. Bouchard?" She paused. "What a pleasant surprise."

"My God, you look great, Helen!"

Sis looked at her mother and for the first time that day noticed that she did look very nice. She had on a simple navy-blue suit, belted at the waist, showing off her still striking figure. Her white blouse was buttoned at the top, with a narrow red satin tie under the collar and tied in front. She wore matching red pumps, and she was carrying her red leather clutch. This was her mother's best dress outfit. She had never worn it to go shopping before.

"Who's this young woman? I don't remember a younger sister. She's the spitting image of you."

Both Helen and Sis were amused. They heard this line a lot. Mechanics, butchers, salesmen, especially magazine salesmen, were always "mistaking" them for sisters. But Sis thought that this man, with his smooth, full, newscaster's voice, made it sound sincere. Quite charming.

Then his eyes caught hers, and he was appraising her from head to toe. Her mother had taken his outstretched hand.

"Mr. Bouchard, let me introduce you to my daughter, Sis. Honey, this is Mr. Crane Bouchard, a close friend of your Grandpa Hecht's."

"Congressman Bouchard, Helen, dear," he said, smiling broadly.

"Congressman Bouchard," Helen repeated, smiling back. "Who would think that a little Mississippi River town girl like me would ever know a congressman?"

Sis was so embarrassed, she wanted to turn and run. She could not believe her mother was playing up to this stranger.

"Now Helen, you know as well as I do that if your father had lived longer, he would have been in the Congress himself."

"I like to think so," Helen said.

"He showed me the ropes, introduced me to his friends. He helped me a great deal."

"What happened between you?"

"It's too many years ago to remember."

Congressman . . . congressman . . . Sis thought. Then she remembered why he looked familiar. There was a picture of him in the Sunday *Post-Dispatch* the previous week. She even remembered the caption. "Congressman Crane Bouchard Seen About Town at Pat's Place." The article mentioned his recent retirement but said that he was found most weekdays at Pat's Place for lunch and afternoon visiting.

Sis probably wouldn't have noticed it, but Helen had folded the paper underneath, so the picture showed clearly, and set it aside by itself. When Sis glanced at it, her mother started to put it away. Sis remembered saying," That guy kind of reminds me of an older, fatter John Kennedy."

"Yes, he does, doesn't he?" Helen said.

Congressman Bouchard and Helen were still talking quietly. Yet, Sis noticed that while the man had her mother's undivided attention, he was only half listening to Helen. His gaze kept returning to Sis, and Helen was so wrapped up in her own agenda that she didn't notice.

The maître d' ushered them to a choice window-side table in the bar. Crane suggested having a drink together before lunch. Sis noticed that he was well-known here, certainly they all treated him with deference. Although with this closer look at him, Sis felt his appearance was unsuited for the place. His tailored suit was rumpled, and his expensive shoes were dull with neglect.

The congressman personally seated each of them, putting Sis in the seat next to his. Sis moved forward slightly as his chest nudged her shoulder when he seated her.

"I just can't believe that you have such a grown-up young woman for a daughter, Helen," he said, looking Sis's way. His more and more intense sideways glances were making her quite uncomfortable. "You're barely old enough to have a daughter."

Helen beamed at Crane as he poured on the charm.

"And she's so pretty. The world will open up for you, young lady," he said, turning directly to Sis. "You can have whatever you want out of life."

For that instant, under Crane's intense scrutiny, Sis sensed his open admiration, and this was even more unsettling than his practiced charm.

"I'll be happy if she just meets a good man with a secure income and settles down," Helen said.

Ignoring Helen, Crane kept talking to Sis. "Do you realize how lovely you are?" he asked.

Sis blushed, but Crane's words, spoken so casually, nonchalantly brushed away the years of hearing Helen tell her she wasn't special. She was smart, but like all other girls, she wanted to be pretty, even beautiful. And more than anything else she wanted to be famous, even more famous than her mother dreamed possible for Grandpa Hecht. Her own mother didn't think she was pretty enough, or special enough, but Crane did. He said so.

"Crane, don't fill her head with thoughts like that." Helen leaned forward a bit and lightly touched Crane's hand on the cocktail table. He didn't seem to notice. He was watching Sis, his eyes lowered to her neck and then her bust. The intimacy startled Sis out of her reverie and she flinched.

Before anyone spoke again, a cocktail waitress, dressed in a short black skirt, walked up to Crane. "How are you doing today? Can I get you something from the bar? Your usual maybe?"

Sis thought they seemed to know each other quite well, but Helen paid little attention. The waitress stood close enough for him to move his left hand around behind her and rest it on her hip.

"Sure, honey. My usual. Plus a glass of your best wine for the lovely lady across the table and a Shirley Temple for this lovely young lady at my right."

"I'd rather have plain soda." Sis asserted. "A coke please."

"Well, I've never known you to make a mistake with a lady," the waitress said with a flip of her head. "Who gets the check, sir?"

"Put it on my tab!"

"Your tab? Oh, yes, of course. By the way, Jake has a message for you. A phone call I believe. I'm sorry I forgot to tell you sooner."

"Sure. I'll be there in a minute. Ladies, will you excuse me? While I'm gone, why don't you two consider coming back to St. Louis soon and having lunch with me here? I have an early afternoon appointment, or I'd stay today. Probably what this call's about."

After Crane was out of earshot, Helen nudged her daughter. "He wants to see us again!"

"You don't want to see him, do you?"

"He's a great man. A Congressman."

"Okay, but why don't you just plan to come by yourself?"

"That would be selfish of me," Helen smiled as if she knew a secret the rest of the world didn't know.

"Mom, did you know this guy would be here today?"

"What gave you that idea?"

"An article in the Post about a month ago. You planned this, didn't you? You came here on purpose to see that old . . . old creep?"

"How dare you talk like that? If your dad were here, he'd probably have a few words to say to you."

"If dad were here, he'd be busy 'saying a few words' to you for playing footsie with this guy."

"And he'd be a damned hypocrite too."

"Come on, Mom. The truth. Was he expecting us?"

"No."

"He knew your married name."

"I did it for you."

"For me, how for me?"

"I thought I might renew a friendship with him," Helen said, looking across the dining room towards Crane as if she could will him to come back to them. "Then, he might introduce us to some of his friends, perhaps an up-and-coming young attorney, or two."

"You can't mean it?"

"Why not? You can't marry a rich man if you never meet one."

Crane was walking back to the table, he seemed agitated. As he sat down, Sis moved her chair a few more inches to the right, away from him. Helen was trying to glare at Sis and flirt with Crane at the same time. The waitress came back with the drinks and the check. Crane paid her with cash, counting the change out to the penny.

The waitress looked amused. "Stiffed me, huh. Well, I guess it's not the first time," she said with a wink.

God, he's sleeping with her, Sis thought.

When Helen Wasilec finally had Crane's attention, she cocked her head to one side and said, "If you'd like, Crane, we could come back next Saturday."

"Superb, Helen. It's settled, ladies. And after dinner, I'll take you both out for an evening dance on the Admiral Steam wheeler."

"Sorry, guys. I can't come next weekend," Sis said. "But I'm sure you'll have a good time without me."

"Nonsense," Crane said rising, with a smug look that told Sis that he always got his way. "You don't want to disappoint your mother, do you?"

He had her there, Sis never wanted to add to her mother's disappointment in life.

"Think of what fun we'll have!" Crane was effusive, looking down at Sis. "And to make it special, I'll save the last dance for you, Honey."

"What?" Helen asked, jarred into awareness.

"I'll save the last dance for Sis, so she'll come with us."

Sis waited for her mother's reply, which was slow coming as if her words, whatever they would be, were held suspended somewhere out of the reach of her tongue. *Tell him we don't need him. We don't, Mom. Tell him to get lost!*

"For Sis?" Helen said, the shock was still registering, and Helen again seemed unable to speak. A long forty seconds later, she regained her voice, though it was barely audible. "Well, yes, of course."

When Sis heard her mother's reply, her mind amplified Helen's words until they roared in her ears.

"Of course, she'll be there," Helen was back in control. "Whatever it is she's got planned, she'll change it."

Crane rose from his seat and moved toward Sis, who stiffened in her chair as he leaned over and wrapped her in a goodbye hug, leaving behind only a stale smell of his alcohol drenched breath when he left. Sis saw her mother look after him as if he were a disappearing dream.

Somehow, they were on the street again. Sis recognized a confused look her mother sometimes got, making her whole expression wistful, not strong and down to earth like she generally was.

"He used to sit on the sun porch with your grandpa, their big cigars smoking up the whole back of the house. Mother hated it, but I loved the smell. I felt safe when Grandpa was home."

"That was then, Mother. Grandpa is dead."

"Crane's not that much older than I am really. Six years or so. You know he gave me my first real kiss." She turned to Sis. "It was the year before I met your father."

Sis wished she could help her mother, try to get her to see Crane for what he was.

"It was my sixteenth birthday and when Crane found out he rushed out in the garden and picked me a beautiful pink rose in full bloom. When he gave it to me, he pulled me to him and kissed me so hard on the lips I had to catch my breath."

"Mom, you don't have to tell me this."

"He would have kissed me again, I know he would, but Grandpa sent me into the house for some whiskey. Grandpa was furious with him for kissing me, but I was delirious. A month or so later, he stopped coming by. Your grandpa said they had a political falling out. It happens."

Helen took a deep breath and sighed. "I didn't see him again until Grandpa died. I was so upset then, I couldn't think of anything else but that my Pops was gone. How would I know it was the last time I'd see Crane too. But I never forgot him. Or that pink rose."

Sis saw the familiar flow of happy remembrance that always came over her mother when she talked about Grandpa Hecht. Before Crane, Sis had felt her mother deserved to take what pleasure she could in memory. But now, her mother seemed as grotesque as Blanche Dubois, dreaming of her young lover, always depending on the "kindness of strangers."

Sis tried to get Helen's mind back to reality. "Grandpa Hecht is dead, Mom, and Dad may be a mold maker, but he bought us this lunch. We don't need Crane Bouchard."

They walked silently for awhile, then Helen stopped, quietly looking at something in her hand. A moment later she was fluttering a rectangular piece of paper before her daughter's eyes. "Will you look at this? He gave us his address and private phone number on a blank check."

"Mom."

"He wants to help us," Helen said.

"He's not interested in helping us."

"He is, don't you see? He's telling me with this check."

"He's probably too broke to buy cards, besides, it's voided and not signed."

"Remember what he said? You can have anything you want." Helen's voice was exuberant.

Sis felt a familiar throbbing behind her eyes, above her jaw, and in her forehead.

"Sis, you can be somebody! Maybe even Mrs. Crane Bouchard. With Crane's money, you can read and write your plays until you're blue in the face. And I won't have to worry about you ending up living in your sister's house."

"I don't have a sister."

"Any relative's house."

"Mom."

Helen didn't stop to listen. "Sissy, baby, it's your chance. The one I never had, or maybe did have, but your grandpa threw it away for me. It's here all over again; only it's for you this time."

Sis grabbed her mother's arm to stop her, to physically make her pay attention.

"This is crazy. You can't mean it."

Wrenching her arm out of Sis's grasp, Helen glared at her daughter. "Why not? Don't you think you're special enough to get a man like Crane? I'll get him for you."

"You're talking crazy, Mom." Sis Wasilec fell back away from her mother and walked more slowly, watching their reflection in the store windows. The other woman in the window looked like her mother, but Sis did not recognize the person she loved. *How could you even think of letting that lecherous old bastard touch me!*

The woman just kept walking and talking. She paused at one of the jewelry stores. "Real diamonds, real gold, no costume jewelry for you."

Sis moved even more slowly behind Helen, who kept on speaking, "I wonder if Crane still drives a Cadillac. Probably that or a Lincoln. Your grandpa always admired a Lincoln."

The VIP Travel signs seemed cold and flat as they approached them. Sis heard her mother's voice. "Look at that Hawaii poster. That's a real possibility."

Sis did not answer. Helen Wasilec stopped. They looked into the cold glass window together. Mother and daughter, light-skinned and blonde, were reflected, oddly mixed in with the poster's lifeless, smiling images of tanned tourists and brown-skinned natives on the beach.

After a few seconds, Helen turned to the window of the Oriental Bazaar Import Shop, her eye caught by something in the display. "Sis, that elephant carving is ivory. I thought it was illegal to bring ivory out of Africa now!" Helen was moving down the sidewalk again.

Sis paused a moment to look at the carving, she heard her mother's voice, but she couldn't seem to follow.

"Didn't I tell you?"

Farther away now, Helen's voice still reached Sis, despite the sounds of the city, Helen's words echoing in Sis's ears. "Anything." The hot summer sunlight bounced off the shop windows reflecting an image of the steaming St. Louis Street. "You can buy absolutely anything here."

Sis turned to the display window of the Oriental Bazaar and saw herself.

Arthur's Bluff
Alton, IL — 1960s

Riverview Park, one hundred feet up on the Mississippi River bluffs above Alton, Illinois, was a favorite partying place for high school students before 10:00 PM and college students later in the night. Alone with Arthur Newstead, who was not only her lover's best friend, but an extremely attractive young black man, Sis felt anxious and uncertain. In 1962 it was chic for white college girls to date black college boys, but it could be dangerous if they were seen. Sis admitted that there was sexual tension between Arthur and her from time to time, but she ignored it. This was not a date, just a friendly visit to console themselves over missing Ted Fox, who once more had been sent to the family farm in Springfield, ostensibly to help his ninety-two-year-old grandfather, but actually to try to kick the amphetamine addiction he developed working as an orderly on night shifts at the hospital.

During a previous visit of Ted's to help his grandfather on the farm, Sis and Arthur did try a double date with Angie Jurgemeister, a white girlfriend of Sis's, and William Johnson, a black friend of Arthur's. They were all in the "artsy" group on campus. A double date in Alton with two racially mixed couples meant drinking in a parked car somewhere or finding a remote spot like this park, where the likelihood of being harassed by the police or being attacked by rednecks was lessened.

That night it rained, so they parked in the lot with the "day glo" signs that read, "Park closes at 10:00 PM." It was after ten, but they were in the car—Angie and William in the front with Arthur and Sis in the back. After drinking three-fourths of a bottle of Thunderbird wine among them, Angie and William were making out.

Arthur and Sis were talking about Ted, their usual subject. The moonlight and the rain that slid down the front windshield made shining silver rivulets on the glass. Angie's and William's heads together as they kissed were silhouetted against the pane of light.

"I wish we were as innocent as they are," Sis said.

"Yeah, I think they're both virgins," Arthur answered.

"Only virgins could kiss like that and not go further," Sis added.

"Oh yeah babe, if we tried that we'd be naked in the sheets in an hour."

Sis sat closer to him, the back of her neck touching the inside of the arm he was resting on the back of the seat. "We probably shouldn't kiss at all," she said.

"Right on, baby, I know I wouldn't stop."

"Arthur, if we had met before Ted and I met, do you think we might have been lovers?"

"Who knows about love. I do know if we were lovers, I'd leave you some time or other."

"I don't believe you would, not if you loved me."

"Racially mixed couples have a fucking hard time, and you, you're too easy. You'd do anything I wanted you to. If we ever got low on money, and I couldn't buy booze or dope, I'd put you out on the street."

Sis's arms pulled together against her sides in an uncontrollable shiver of repulsion at what Arthur had just said. "You wouldn't."

"I wish that were true, babe. But the truth is I would. No matter how you see it, William there and me live in a whole different world from you and Angie and Ted."

• • •

Angie and William ran away to get married two weeks later, but after a month went by with no word, Angie came home alone, pregnant. Nobody had heard from William since.

Arthur and Sis continued to play it cool. That was easy because Ted came back about the same time Angie did, so whenever Arthur and Sis were together, they were with their mutually loved Ted Fox.

• • •

Arthur's voice was calling her from across the forbidden wall, giving Sis that same rush of living on the edge she got from being with Ted.

"Come on, it's safe. See, even with my legs stretched out there's at least a foot or more before I'd be at the edge." Arthur was six foot two with long legs. "If there's room for me there's room for you, short stuff."

For the first time since she met him, Sis wondered if he'd played basketball when he was at Alton High. Tall black boys always went out for basketball. If a black boy was stocky and heavyset, he played football. The year before when Sis was a senior, the Alton High Redbirds football team had so many negro players that people around town started calling them the Alton High Blackbirds. Sis's mother had been very upset when Joe Sr. repeated that name at home.

I don't think he ever talks about sports, Sis thought. When they were running together as a threesome—Sis, Ted, and Arthur, Ted and Arthur talked about Blake, Eliot, Miles Davis,

Nietzsche, the Modern Jazz Quartet, and new ways to get high. The latter was always at the top of their list. One evening they spent four hours talking about plans for getting bulk methedrine powder from a scientific supply company that Ted knew about from his night job at the hospital. Arthur and Ted were both college seniors. They met as freshmen in Al Archer's class at Southern Illinois University's Alton Residence Center.

"Hey baby, what's the hold up?" Arthur called, as Sis measured the height of the wall against her waist. Her legs were short, but strong. "What you scared of?"

"Nothing!" She said as she climbed up and threw one leg over the top of the wall.

"The boogie man, maybe," he said, grinning, showing a mouthful of white teeth gleaming at her in the dark.

"God, Arthur, stop that, you look like Satchmo."

"A spade's a spade." Arthur said, the Satchmo grin still in place.

"Fuck you!" She knew that was what he was waiting to hear so he could give his trademark answer.

"Why not?" Arthur would say, stretching the sounds out in a seductive low-pitched tone. This usually ended whatever disagreement had elicited the expletive, especially if it was said during a fight or by another guy.

But the first time Arthur said, "Why not?" to her, with that challenge in his great dark eyes, Sis had retorted in a disparaging tone, "Why?"

This was the perfect answer to his perfect answer, and they became friends.

"Why?" she called as she hopped off the wall and walked over to sit down next to him. "That's right, baby, just keep asking ole Uncle Arthur why and someday I'm gonna show you," Arthur challenged again.

"I'd probably be better off with you than Ted," she was sitting with her knees pulled up to her chin, hands clasped round her legs.

"You are definitely better off without that stupid bastard when he's crazy high, but I'm no better. Never, ever think that," Arthur said, punctuating the statement by pointing his right forefinger at her. "Remember what I said about putting you out on the street. I meant it baby!"

Sis did think she might be better off with Arthur though. He had protected her from Ted more than she cared to remember. The most recent incident was just before Ted's parents whisked him off to Springfield.

Ted's paranoia from using amphetamines was getting out of control. Sis had become increasingly fearful of leaving Ted alone because she never knew what she would find when she got home. One night she came home to a living room strewn with their books. Ted and Arthur were crawling back and forth in front of the now empty bookcases listening for voices.

"Ted, there's no one there. There couldn't be," Sis said.

"They are there, and you know it. You hear them too."

"The wall isn't thick enough for people to hide behind. I wouldn't lie to you."

"You would if you were working for them," Ted's voice was menacing. His eyes were wild. She saw his hand reach for something under the green fringed cushion on the apartment's floor.

"God, Ted, no!" Sis said. "Where did you get that? It's not loaded, is it?"

The gun was pointed directly at her face. "You'd better believe it's loaded, bitch! You'd better stop lying about the voices."

"I'm not lying, Ted. I can't hear them." Ted was still aiming the gun at her head.

Thinking quickly, Arthur moved toward the bookcases, bending down. "Hey, man. Cool it. Maybe she's just not close enough to hear the voices."

Throughout the rest of the night, Arthur, Ted, and Sis crawled around the baseboards of Sis's three-room apartment, listening to the voices. Finally, Ted got up and calmly said they seemed to have gone away. Sis and Arthur concurred, then Sis rocked Ted in her arms until the sunrise, when she had to dress for work.

Although Sis's family did not know about this incident, Helen Wasilec was worried for her daughter. No amount of coaxing or cajoling could convince Sis to leave Ted. Yet, it was Sis being seen with Arthur that had caused the biggest rift in the Wasilec family.

"Nice girls do not run around with two boys." Helen Wasilec was as close to yelling at her daughter as she had ever been. "And especially not a black boy."

"They're not boys, Mom," Sis smarted back. "They are both twenty-one. That makes them men."

"Boys or men, they're both no good, especially that . . . that . . ."

"What?"

"You know."

"No, I don't know, Mom. You weren't going to say nigger were you? You, the sainted Helen Wasilec, who single-handedly integrated the third grade of Horace Mann School. You wouldn't call anyone that word, would you?"

"You're just doing this to embarrass me, embarrass your dad, even your poor Aunt Phil who can't show her face to her friends. Everyone in town knows about this."

"As big as Alton is, I think that might be a slight exaggeration."

"I'm not exaggerating. Mildred Kaufman told me she saw you riding around with them in the front seat of your car, that awful Ted Fox boy driving, you in the middle, and that black boy on the other side, pushed right up against you."

Helen's face registered how distasteful this was to her. Sis knew she was really hurt, but she couldn't stop herself from one more jab before she walked out of the kitchen into her room and slammed the door.

"Somebody I used to respect taught me to see people for who they are, not what they are. Not to care about race or money or position or religion. I guess she was lying to me all along."

Sis left her mother standing alone in the small kitchen, a lit cigarette falling off the edge of an ashtray onto the tile floor, leaving another one of hundreds of burn marks that were scattered throughout the house.

Sis wondered why she thought of that now. Was she here, alone with Arthur, partly to spite her mother, or to prove something to both of them.

"How long did Ted say he'd be gone this time?" Arthur said.

"He didn't. Just said his folks wanted him to go to Springfield to help his grandpa with the farm. You know what that means," Sis said. "I hope he'll be back before the semester starts."

"That's a long time. He'll be back sooner."

"Yeah, what makes you think so?"

"Well, as soon as he's clean, he's going to start missing his big breasted blond."

"Or my prescription for diet pills," Sis said.

"You don't think he'd come back for sex alone, like in your song. Hey, sing it for me."

"Ted hates that song."

"Well, Ted is not here, is he?"

"Rub it in," Sis said.

"Why not?"

"No, I don't feel like it," Sis said.

"Sure you do. Here, have a swig of this?" Arthur reached behind his back and then swung a bottle of Silver Satin in front of her.

"That's make out wine," she said. "I've heard you tell Ted you use that on all your women, that it's an aphrodisiac."

"It's cheap wine. Couldn't get Thunderbird tonight, and I wanted to try something white," Arthur said with a slight smile.

"Well, drink it yourself." Sis stretched her legs out now and was sitting with her hands behind her back.

"If you won't sing for me, at least have a drink with me."

"Okay, I'll have a drink with you." Sis took a long drag off the bottle.

Then Arthur raised the bottle and took another swig of the wine. "Sheeeeeeeeitt!" Arthur crooned the way Ted did. "Here's to you, Ted!"

Arthur passed the bottle to Sis again. This time she just pretended to drink some, then passed it back. She learned long ago not to try to keep up with Ted or Arthur.

"You know he loves you as much as he can love anyone." Arthur said, lying back down in the grass.

"I've heard that before."

"Ted told you that he loved you?"

"No, our dear drunken English prof, Al Archer, who leches after anyone who moves, told me."

"Al Archer loves you?"

"Cut it out," Sis said. "Al Archer loves everyone, probably you, too. No, Al told me that Ted loves me, and just like you did, clarified it with 'as much as he loves anyone.'"

"Well, Al knows him pretty well."

"Then Al told me that Ted didn't love anyone, especially himself. So, if you follow the logic, Ted doesn't love me," Sis said. "I got the short end of the stick again."

"I hear Ted's stick isn't short," Arthur said.

"Yeah, well it's not here either."

"Have a swig."

"No, we'd better get back."

"I've got some pot," Arthur said.

"Pot, did you have something planned?"

"I've always got pot," Arthur said.

"Don't smoke it, please. I really am not in the mood to get picked up by any of these hot dog Alton policemen tonight."

"Cuz you're out with a coon?"

Something about this teasing dig really pissed Sis off. "Jesus, stop it! I've heard just about enough of your playing poor little colored boy tonight." The words were out before she realized it.

"And I've had all I can take of your white-bitch, everybody's-equal crap. You don't have the least idea about me or my life or what it's like to be colored."

"Damn, Arthur, you pass all the time. Your skin is barely darker than mine." Sis was on her feet, yelling at him. "You just like to play the poor downtrodden . . ."

"Go on you bitch, say it!" Arthur's voice was terrifyingly calm. He took another swig.

"God, Arthur, I'm sorry." Sis was kneeling down beside him, reaching over to touch him, somehow reach him, when she felt the pain and heard the sound of the back of Arthur's long fingered hand hitting against the side of her face. He slapped her so hard she fell over backwards, towards the edge of the cliff, cracking her head soundly against the sun-hardened ground. She lay there stunned.

He made no apologies as she slowly raised herself to a sitting position, the side of her face swelling and painful. The wind was knocked out of her, and tears were streaming onto the dusty ground, making small bubbles of liquid that lay on the earth. She was shaking, crying but not making a sound.

He just lay back on his side, looking at her, then down at the river.

After three or four endless minutes, he got up and walked over to her, taking her one hand in his, then the other, pulling her up. When she was on her feet, still shaking, he turned her around facing the edge of the bluff and the water, a good half mile away, but it looked like it was right next to the edge from their perspective.

A three-quarters full moon made a long curving reflection in the middle of the river that went on for miles. He was standing behind her now, both arms around her, holding her by the wrists. He raised her arm and pointed it toward the reflection.

"What do you see?"

Too frightened to talk, she didn't answer.

"Come on, baby, what do you see? Answer me!"

"The river," She cleared her throat. "The river reflecting the moonlight."

"What's it mean to you?"

"What?" her voice was thin, lessened somehow.

"Well, is it ugly, pretty, romantic?"

"It's beautiful," she whispered.

"How is it beautiful?" he asked. She was silent. He tightened his hold on her. "How is it beautiful?" His voice was a menacing distortion of his usually soft speech. "Answer the question, what do you see?" He squeezed her wrists harder.

"Arthur, please, you're hurting me."

"Describe what you see, dammit!"

"It's beautiful, uh . . . because of the way the white light reflected off the moon shimmers against the dark water."

"I see a white snake," Arthur said, emphasizing every word. "That snake is growing and growing and growing, and it's trying to swallow all the colored peoples of the world into its already full belly."

A sudden warm breeze wafted over them, but Sis felt only the icy coldness of her fear. Arthur still had her trapped in his arms. She could feel his breath on her neck. Her teeth began to chatter. The noise was loud, like a woodpecker on a quiet morning. She was afraid Arthur would hear it and sense her terror even more.

Stop this, she thought. *He mustn't see how frightened you are. Yeah, well he's already seen that. What would Ted do if he were here?*

Arthur let go of her wrist, knocking her away from him toward his right side. He was staring at the river, transfixed. "Giant white snake, no matter how big you are, we're going to slit you open someday."

Sis was terrified. Ted would make a joke about this being the type of stuff you have to expect when you're out with a spade, but maybe not even Ted could joke Arthur out of this mood. Sis was not going to try. Arthur moved a step forward toward the edge.

Sis, her breath recovered, started toward him. "Arthur."

He took another step.

"Arthur, is that what you think of Ted and me?" she said, reaching for his shirtsleeve, to grab hold of him, to stop him. "Are we just part of that hate?"

He pulled his arm away violently and took another step forward. He was at the edge now, looking out across to the water.

"Arthur, please stop, you're frightening me."

Turning around, he grinned at her, a wide, grotesque grin.

"You stupid white bitch. You are out with a nigger who is whacked out on juice and weed! You should be frightened. I want you to be frightened!"

"Why are you doing this?"

"What?"

"Treating me like this. I'm your friend. I care about you, love you."

"Oh, isn't that fine? All you educated white bitches think your sweet, sweet love solves it all."

"Please stop. I've learned my lesson," Sis's voice was firmer than she believed it could be. "Let's go home."

"Where is home?"

"Anywhere I can get some ice on my face, it really hurts."

"Go on, you go home."

"I can't leave you here."

"Why not?" he said.

"Why?" It was the right thing to say.

That night, Arthur and Sis did the only thing they knew that could make up for the emptiness they both felt without Ted. Sis lay under Arthur on the worn stuffed couch in his room in his family's home. She slid the tips of her fingers over Arthur's maple syrup skin, over the few soft hairs on his back, and thought of Ted's body, soft red hairs at the small of his back. Arthur kissed her, savoring her from her neck to the inside of her thighs, burying his smooth, whiskerless face in her, then moving up and inside, slowly, painstakingly, not like Ted's hard, deep thrusts, but with circular motions, moving with her, taking her away, taking her to the edge, and over.

The next morning, Arthur's fifteen-year-old brother, Martin, woke them before he left for school, and Sis discovered that his bed was in the same room. All Sis could think about for days was Martin, listening, perhaps pleasuring himself, then later, laughing, telling his friends about how Arthur got his best friend's white piece to come home with him and screwed her all night right there in their room with Martin not ten feet away.

At first, when Ted got back, he avoided his old friends, then things went back to normal. Together again as a three-some, they drank and got high, but Sis avoided going with Ted to Arthur's home, even though she was quite fond of his family, especially his mother. Whenever they were there, her shame became all encompassing, not because she expressed her love for Arthur. but because she had not understood the rules of his world.

Our Mothers' Ghosts
St. Louis, MO-Alton, IL — 1965-1990

I cringe whenever I hear the expression, back from the dead. It's such a misconception. How can you come back when you've never gone away? I can say that authoritatively now, having died quite recently. Some spirits do go away, but with the exception of those who go directly to Hell, each individual spirit has to decide to go or to stay. If you go, the next stage is a period of rest and growth without the hindrance of bodily functions. Most spirits make the decision based on emotion, not wanting to leave a loved one, dying too young, dying just short of some accomplishment, wanting to wreak vengeance on someone, or just not being ready and not knowing for sure why. I wasn't ready. I was sorely tempted to leave, unsure about whether I would have to stay wherever my husband had my body buried or whether I'd be totally free of it.

Something inside me—excuse the expression, spirits do have a spatial form, a little depth—said, "Hang around. They're going to need you." I had not one clue as to how "they" would need me or who "they" were, but I felt sure they were my youngest son, my daughter, and my sister, Boots. That was enough for me. To be completely honest, I think I knew I still needed them as well.

In any new situation, you have to adjust, and though I did like the idea of not having a body to contend with, mine had worn out quite early and given me problems for a decade. It took me a while to truly appreciate the full potential of being a spirit. When I did, I immediately thought of several things I might do, things that I hadn't gotten to do in the fifty-two years of my life as daughter, sister, friend, woman, wife, and mother. I might finally learn to play the piano well. What fun it would be to make a piano play with no visible pianist. Then there were the midnight swims at Blue Pool that I could join. My widowed mother always impressed upon my sister Boots and I that Blue Pool was definitely off limits.

"The current and undertow are too strong. It can pull you down to the caves below and suck you right out into the river." My mother's exact words, her hair in a tight gray bun, her face in a grimace. "You'd be lost forever!" She never failed to exaggerate our potential doom or punishments.

Despite mother's warning, Boots went to Blue Pool many times and did not get sucked into anything but an early pregnancy and a disastrous marriage. I was the respectable sister, always more respectable than Boots.

"Prissy! Don't ask Miss Prissy, she might get her dress dirty, or mess up her curls," Boots would chide as she headed off into the quarries for target shooting with the Hayes boys. She was right, I did like to keep perfectly clean and well-kept. I had to be to please our mother. While Boots was off being an adventurous tomboy, I stayed at home and played the perfect daughter. We were like two sides of a record, always opposite and complementing types of songs, one, perhaps more popular, but neither able to spin on the turntable without the other.

Growing up we never thought about how important we were to each other. It was only after we were in high school that I realized how much Boots did for me. She always took the blame, no matter how small or how large the offense. I'm not sure she meant to, but it happened that way.

"Boots, did you drag that mud into the house?" Mom would say, her voice cold and threatening. Or if the chickens were squawking into the morning, "Boots, did you forget to feed the chickens again?" Or, "How many times have I told you not to let those Hayes brats into this yard!" Boots never told on me, when I was the one who forgot the chickens, or brought in the mud, or let any of the neighborhood children into our yard.

We grew up like this, fulfilling our roles to the hilt. I was the good daughter and Boots was the black sheep.

Boots was by my side the night I died. It was New Year's Eve 1965. Boots's previous New Year's Eve carryings-on were legend in our family because she was a celebratory person, and December 31st was also her birthday. In her forties she married for the third time. Macon was a man not given to the kinds of celebrations Boots had known, but a good man and this marriage was a take. After that, we always celebrated New Year's Eve together, at least the three of us. By then, my husband Joe had started carousing and was never around. I liked being with my sister on her birthday. That's why I picked that night to die. I knew she would be with me, and that she would want to be. She looked bone tired as she sat there. Her wispy, dull blond hair, her quiet blue eyes, her middle-aged face, the picture of me when I was healthy.

"I called Sis. She will leave first thing in the morning and be here by noon," Boots said, squeezing my hand. I was pleased that my daughter was coming but I didn't want to wait for her. I didn't want her there when I did it. She was one of the reasons I had held onto life for so long, the other was the joy of life itself.

"Can you hear me?" Boots asked. I blinked twice. Imperceptively, I guess, because she didn't get the signal.

"I hope you hear me," she said, then stood up slowly and leaned over to kiss my forehead. I had no control at all over any part of my body except my eyelids, but no one seemed to notice the movements I made with them. So, when Boots kissed me, I closed them tight to enjoy the feel of her warm caress more fully in the dark comfort of the room.

A door opened, I heard my husband's voice, gruff and deep, but not characteristically loud. He hardly ever spoke below a shout at home. He was standing in the doorway. I sensed that he dreaded coming in, but it was almost his shift, 11:15 PM. "I just wanted to tell you I'm here," he said to Boots. Several days before, Joe had accepted the doctor's assessment that I couldn't hear anything, so he communicated as little to me while I was dying as he had during our marriage. It seemed appropriate.

"You're early," Boots said. "Why don't you go up to the coffee shop and grab a bite to eat? I want to stay my shift." She had gotten up and walked over to the door. Joe left, relieved to be saved even forty-five minutes of his duty. On the way back to my bedside, Boots opened the curtains and stood awhile, looking out on the St. Louis skyline. 1 watched it with her, having gotten some of my spirit abilities already. The lights flickered in the crisp December air and seemed to map the city. The main streets were flowing rivers of light with opposing currents, the blocks marked off, the major buildings pinpointed by light. From our vantage point, twenty-six stories up in Barnes Hospital's Queeny Tower, the New Year was a flurry of silent light.

We returned to my bed. Boots sat down beside me again and began to read, her free right hand holding mine. At exactly 11:48 PM, Central Standard Time, I moved completely out of my body, and it stopped breathing. I felt cold and dislocated looking down on my lifeless body, my warmth still in it. Seconds later Boots realized, hugged me tearfully, and called the nurse's station. She didn't just push the call button. She phoned them.

Within minutes, my room was full of people—two nurses, a doctor, and a Catholic priest who gave my body the last rites. I was surprised at getting such quick service, and me just a convert.

Joe was there by then. He kept thinking, *Fourteen more minutes and I could have claimed you on my income tax. Fourteen more minutes.*

I forgave him. He did have a lot of hospital bills to pay, at least $4,000 over what the insurance paid, and that was for a dead wife.

The funeral was more difficult than I expected. I didn't have much time to practice my spirit skills, so I found going through doors disconcerting. It leaves you feeling fragmented, much the same way fulfilling all the many roles a woman has to play makes you feel. I suppose this feeling is new to male spirits.

It's not easy to hover over a group of people and hear yourself discussed as if you were gone. As time goes by you can actually respond to remarks about yourself by creating a sense of pleasant remembrance for the speaker or by casting a warning chill.

"She's so much better off, dear." Mildred Kaufman, in her best dress, a $15.98 bargain basement item her husband probably picked out, was holding my daughter, Sis's hand. Mildred Kaufman, one of my best friends, saying I was better off dead. What did she know? Well, actually, a lot. I told her a lot that I hid from everyone else but Boots. It was possible Mildred did think I was better off.

"At least she's at rest now." That was my Joe, standing by the coffin, nodding and shaking hands with our family—he had not spoken to two of his brothers in years—friends, neighbors, people we barely knew, and his boss. What a sight that was. Joe hated his boss, but he was smiling, shaking hands, and making comments like, "I can't believe she's gone. My beloved, loving wife."

I guess one part of that was true, I did love Joe.

He was a good provider, and he really couldn't help the way he felt about women. It was all he'd ever seen. Somehow our niece, Mae Ellen, Boots's daughter, was spared this side of Joe. But then she lived with us before I got sick. Sis witnessed and experienced the worst of his harshness and cruelty, which seemed to get worse in direct proportion to my diabetes.

Sis was the one that I was most worried about. She was still standing several feet from my coffin, meeting and greeting my mourners, but I could see her gritting her teeth, and I knew she wanted to scream at her father. I knew the look.

I tried to winnow through all the voices and thoughts I could hear, get to Sis's only, but it was like a kaleidoscope of sound. "She suffered so." "A saint, living with that man." "He's the devil's own partner." "My, goodness, isn't that one of his women?" "At least she doesn't have to face that anymore." "Mama." "I never could stand that man." "God, my feet are killing me." "Mama." "Mama, I'm so sorry, so sorry for everything I caused." Sis's thoughts, those last were Sis's thoughts. "Mama, please forgive me."

Before I died, I thought spirits knew more, had more control over life than the living. But I didn't have a clue as to what Sis meant. Granted, I wasn't happy with her choice of husband. He was too much like her father for my liking. Boots's daughter, Mae Ellen, had married a man like her father, too. Generation after generation, we seemed to make the same mistakes, but I had hoped Sis would break the chain.

My oldest child, Joe Jr., was standing with my youngest, Benny, by the entranceway when Mae Ellen arrived. Boots was visiting with some of our relatives who had come from Grafton for the viewing, and she didn't see Mae Ellen right away. Joe Jr. took Mae Ellen into his arms and hugged her with the brotherly affection he had always felt for this cousin.

"Mae Ellen, it's great to see you."

"You too, Joe, Benny. I'm just sorry it's like this."

"Sis tells me you spent a lot of time with Mom near the end."

"Well, I live closer than either of you."

Mae Ellen and Joe Jr. reminisced about their childhood together, their teens, and the three years Mae Ellen had lived with us while Boots was going through some hard times.

Mae Ellen was actually more like me when I was healthy than Sis was. When Mae Ellen lived with us, I had the patience to teach her the things I had learned from all those years with my mother. Listening to my niece and son talk, I remembered Mae Ellen there in the kitchen with me, her dark brown hair up in a ponytail, her sleeves rolled up, stretching the curtain sheers on a frame, carefully avoiding the sharp needle points that stuck up from the wood to hold the curtain in place. She knew that if she pricked her fingers and got blood on the curtain, it would have to be washed and stretched again.

I taught her to polish the furniture until you could see your face in it, how to take care of roses, and how to care for her sweet babies, her little boy, Robert, with his great brown eyes, Melinda with her blond curls, and the sweetest of all, Carrie, who looked just like Mae Ellen had when she was a baby. I never knew her other children, but I loved these like a grandmother.

I was startled back from these memories by the sound of Sis's crying. I could hear it above the din of everyone talking, but I couldn't quite tell where she was. I wished spirit hearing was easier to focus.

I hovered close to Benny's ears and whispered, "Look for Sis, look for Sis, she needs someone." I don't know why I whispered. Nobody could hear me, even if I had yelled. I didn't have any power to communicate yet. What use was it to be there if I couldn't help my own daughter.

Where was she? Focusing my energies on Sis's quiet sobs, I finally noticed a curtained-off alcove to the left of the casket. It was meant as a private viewing place for the closest family. I only had to see it, think I wanted to be there, and I was there.

Sis was sitting on a cushioned loveseat with Boots, who had her arm around her, comforting her.

"I should have been there, Aunt Boots. I should have stayed here in Alton with her instead of moving up to Chicago."

I had never seen Boots look so maternal. She was gently smoothing Sis's hair as she held her. "Your mom understood, honey."

"I hope so Aunt Boots. I tried to write her every day, but Harry and I just didn't have the money to come home much."

"You were home at Thanksgiving. She was so happy to see you then."

"We didn't stay long."

"And you were here at Christmas."

"She didn't know me then. I thought she did, but Dr. Banks told me she was in too deep a coma to hear or recognize anyone."

"Did you believe that?"

"No, not at first. At first I thought she was responding to me, blinking her eyes to signal yes and no." Sis was sitting up straight on the loveseat, getting a Kleenex out of her purse.

"And then Banks tested her sense of feel on the bottoms of her feet with a needle, stabbing her feet. I wanted to scream at him to leave her alone."

"I know, honey. I felt that way, too."

"I hated him almost as much as Dad, going on and on about the bills, asking Banks how much longer she could be like that, just lying there, more dead than alive." Sis's blue eyes were red and swollen, her sobs interfering with her ability to talk. "I'll never forgive Dad for treating her the way he did, and I'll never forgive myself for leaving her alone with him."

"Wait, a minute young lady, I know Helen wouldn't want that." Boots said, looking over at my coffin. "She regained her consciousness for almost a day, just after Christmas, and she forgave your dad. I was there."

"And I wasn't," Sis sobbed. "Dr. Banks said she'd never regain consciousness, or 1 would have stayed. I would have stayed."

"I told her you had been there and were on your way back!"

"It's not the same," Sis had leaned back into the crook of Boots's arm and was crying softly again. "Aunt Boots, I'm pregnant, and I didn't even get to tell Mama. She won't ever know. She won't ever see her grandchildren. Why did I wait so long to decide? And then it took so long."

I could barely stand to see my daughter in such pain. What could I do? How could I help her? Help Boots help her?

Just at that moment, I saw Mae Ellen and Joe Jr. looking around for Boots. And I had the answer. All I had to do was make them remember so strongly that they would reminisce in front of Sis. But first they had to find her. I hovered in front of them, thinking, *In front, in front, behind the curtain*, as hard as I could. It seemed to work. They were heading towards the alcove where Boots and Sis were still talking.

"There you are, Mom. Joe Jr. and I have been looking all over for you two." Mae Ellen's voice was light with happy memories. "Robert and the girls will be here for the funeral. I know Aunt Helen would have liked that."

Perfect. Mae Ellen had said the perfect thing. I knew if I got them all together this could be worked out. Sis would have realized years ago, but Mae Ellen was so much older, they had so little in common. They only saw each other when Mae Ellen visited, and she was much more interested in play-ing with boys than her little girl cousin. Mae Ellen and Joe Jr. both gave Sis big hugs.

"Sis, I hear you and Harry are thinking of moving back closer to Alton soon."

"Yes, I wish Mom had known."

"She did. We talked about it the day she was conscious. The kids and I went up to see her, and she told me you were moving back. She said you told her when you were here at Christmas."

Sis's face brightened, ever so slightly.

"She heard that. Aunt Boots, I told you I thought she could hear me. That stupid doctor said she couldn't." Sis was trying not to cry so she could talk to Mae Ellen.

"Aunt Helen said you were pregnant too. Is it true?"

"I am. I am." Sis's face lit up. "Thank you, Mae Ellen. I'm so happy she knew."

At that Boots broke into the conversation. "She knows. Not she knew. She's probably here with us right now," Boots said. "Remember what your mother told you when Grandma Wasilec died and you cried because they were going to put her in the ground."

Sis answered, wiping away her tears. "Yes, like it was yes-terday. 'That's not Grandma, only her body. Grandma's up in heaven watching over us right now.'"

"Helen is never going to leave any of us as long as we re-member her," Mae Ellen said.

• • •

Sis had a hard time giving birth to that first baby. He was an eight-pound, nine-ounce, twenty-two-inch boy. I was there with her, but it was less than a year after I had died, and I still didn't have enough skill as a ghost to really comfort her. She was in labor two and a half days. The doctor was out of town and the "prince" he had chosen to take his calls didn't want the responsibility of delivering the baby because his head was turned wrong in the birth canal.

Finally on the morning of the third day, I asked Sis's guard-ian angel if she could do something, and she did. The story of the old nurse who came into Sis's room that morning, checked the baby's progress, and said, "This baby has to come out, now!" is a legend in the family.

Although Sis's doctor was back in town, he had called in and said he needed a few hours of sleep. The unit nurse did not want to wake him.

"Call him anyway," the old nurse ordered. "Tell him that Flo said, 'God will let him sleep when he's dead.'"

The night shift had just ended, and all the staff were chang-ing rounds. There was no one to help Flo do any of Sis's final preparations. The old nurse was a small woman, but she was mighty. She pulled a transport bed up to Sis, and although Sis weighed over two hundred pounds pregnant, Flo moved Sis onto the transport by herself. She took Sis to the operating room and transferred her to the operating table by herself. Flo got the anesthetist to start Sis's anesthesia even before the doc-tor had arrived. She held Sis's hand reassuringly as the anesthe-tist put a thick rubber cup over Sis's mouth and asked her to count backward from one hundred. Sis remembers saying "ninety-four."

When Sis first saw her baby, his head was elongated, and his forehead and face had several scratches and bruises. I could feel her love for him as strong as if he were my own and, of course, he was. Even though Mae Ellen's babies had been like grandbabies to me, I was still as excited about little Don as if he were the first.

Sis's doctor finally came into the maternity ward to tell her the details of the birth. "I'm sorry that he looks so bad. The instruments do that every time."

I was wishing I could shut him up. Sis thought her baby was beautiful and now this man was telling her that the baby looked bad.

"You don't have to worry though," he said. "We checked him over thoroughly, and there is no brain damage."

Sis did not go back to "Dr. Tactful" with her second baby. She realized that it was the old nurse's quick action that kept Don from real harm. But, when she tried to find Flo to thank her, neither the doctor nor the other nurses knew who she was, or where she had gone. So, Sis thanked God, and God gave Flo extra stars in her crown.

Two years and two weeks later, Sis was in a labor room again, this time for Megan. Harry was even less empathetic with the second birth than he was with the first. Sis felt so alone that she looked out the window into the darkness of the early morning sky and cried out for me. "Mama, Mama, please help me."

Flo suggested that because I had learned to make myself seen as an anonymous person, I should go in with her.

I stood by Sis and helped her push harder. I comforted her with a wet cloth on her forehead, and reassuring talk. When she told me that it was odd that she called out for her mother because her mother had been dead several years, I told her the truth, "I'm sure she heard, and her spirit is here."

Sis did not remember that I was there at all, but she did remember calling out for me. She said she thought I must have heard her because Megan's birth was easier after that. I'm planning to be there when Megan has her children, too.

When Megan was in her early twenties, she decided to live with her partner, a boy she had met in undergraduate school. She announced this to Sis in a telephone call.

"I know you were hoping I would come home this summer, Mom, but I decided to move in with Andrew and stay in Iowa City. I can earn and save more money here."

"But I didn't know you and Andrew were that serious."

"We've been dating since last summer, Mother."

"Could anything I say, or do, stop you?"

"Not really."

"Just remember, I'm way too young to be a grandma."

Neither of Sis's kids are married yet. Megan isn't even planning to have children. I keep telling Sis, "Be careful what you say. God is always listening."

Time passes so quickly in the spirit world, even if you stay on earth with the mortals. Life got tough for Sis, and I think she appreciated my being around. The divorce was harder than expected. She realized she still loved Harry, but their values were too different to stay together.

He tried to change her mind right up to the last minute. Of course, sleeping with the woman who lived next door to Sis didn't help his case.

Don and Megan were in elementary school when Sis divorced, and I put the idea in Sis's head to start taking them to visit Boots in Alton more. That was good for all of them. Sis took an interest in gardening then, and she brought irises from Boots's garden to plant at her home in Columbia. She had irises in her yard that I had given Boots back in the 1950s.

By the time the kids were grown, Sis had iris beds that rivaled any in Boone County. She really had to juggle her various roles: working mother, student, and writer. She handled everything pretty well except her love life. She had Boots's adventurous nature, with some of her dad's lustfulness thrown in. It didn't seem to bother her that most of the available men she met were already married. She dated both single men and married men, but she always seemed to fall in love with the married ones.

"You know that I try never to interfere," I said to her one night in a dream. She didn't seem surprised to see me at all.

"Sure, Mom," she said.

"I just don't like you seeing that politician—the lobbyist."

"Is he the only one you don't like?"

"Don't you see what a liar he is? You've heard him on the phone to his wife, telling her lies." Sis was squirming in her sleep now. "He lies to you, too."

"I don't care," Sis was talking in her sleep. "I won't ever have to marry him!" she said so loud that she woke herself up.

Though she had more than her fair share of lovers, she never let a man stay over or let the kids see her in bed with anyone. But she could not keep her kids from seeing her cry when each man in turn broke a piece of her heart. After Megan was grown, she told Sis that seeing their mother hurt so often was hard on Don and her. Sis has few regrets, but that is one.

Sis tells her friends she doesn't want to marry again, ever. She's got a stock joke about marriage that she read in a woman's magazine. "Marrying a man is like buying a new piece of furniture. It may look good in the window, but when you get it home, it may not go with the rest of the house." But I think Sis would like to meet a decent single guy that she could build a new life with.

Epilogue

Boots, Sis, and Mae Ellen are here now to see my grave for what I think will be Boots's last Memorial Day visit in her body. Sis has a Prince Albert jonquil in a plastic vial that she wants to put by my grave. Jonquils were among my favorite flowers, along with irises and roses. I saw her planting jonquils in her garden in Columbia. She is my body now. Her hands are mine. They look the same way mine did at her age. She's filling the vial with water from a mud puddle in the drive. I would do that. Mae Ellen is loosening the dirt with a pencil. Her hands are mine, too, and Boots's.

I help Boots back to the car, her back is more bent than ever, and she needs to sit down. Besides, I want our daughters to be alone.

"Mae Ellen, I've been wanting to tell you something," Sis begins. "I just never seem to find the right moment."

"There's nothing you need to tell me."

"I feel like I do," Sis insists. "I never meant to make your mom into a substitute mother for me and grandmother for my kids, but I did."

"I've always thought it was a fair exchange," Mae Ellen answers, putting her arm around Sis and giving her a hug. "Your Mom was my mother when I needed her, and grandmother for my kids, too. Now my mother is yours."

I've been waiting all these years for someone to tell Sis that I never missed a thing. I move closer to Boots and give her a warm hug. She's been thinking about joining me soon, and I let her know I'd like that. I tell her that our mother is even anxious to see her. We have always been a part of one another and soon our spirits will finally be complete.

Letters to Ted
Columbia, MO — 1990s

Sis Wasilec wondered why writing Ted Fox's birthday letter was so difficult the last few years? She spent as much time writing and revising them as she did her stories. In the beginning, before it became a ritual, she sent him a lighthearted card with a brief, friendly note about being over thirty.

Ted responded with a letter recapping his year. It was typed by a secretary, but he signed it himself and added, "Great to hear from you."

Sis sent a card and letter regularly after that. No September passed unacknowledged.

Sis looked up from the page of scratch-outs and rewrites. *I hope he realizes it's just the time of year that makes me think of him,* she thought. *I don't want him to think I have him on my mind a lot. I don't. Not normally at least.*

Soon she would have to move to the end of the table to avoid the bright autumn light in her eyes. A golden maple outside the kitchen window had already lost most of its leaves. The hot, dry summer and violent September storms had taken their toll. *A shame,* she thought.

As Sis reread the final salutation on this latest birthday letter, she mused that it was definitely noncommittal. After fifteen years of being a divorced, single mother, she made it a rule that she must always be noncommittal. The few times she dared to say I love you, or mention next year or the future, the man she was dating called less often and soon faded into history. *I wonder if Ted would have wanted me more*, she thought, *if I had been noncommittal, loved him less.*

Sis read the first paragraph aloud to herself one more time to see if it sounded all right. *Yes, it's innocuous, especially since I deleted "impressionable eighteen," but that describes me perfectly in 1960, the summer 1 fell in love with Ted Fox.*

• • •

Every student, faculty member, and administrator at State College had heard of Ted Fox. He was a published poet and playwright, except for the fact that the head of the English Department at State had ordered his play torn out of every single copy of the spring creative writing magazine because of his constant use of the word "fuck," in all its conjugated forms. The administration's actions made Ted an instant hero to artistic types who had previously considered him a vulgar bore.

There were a few contraband and intact copies of the original magazine around. Sis had not even seen one, but Anna had read it. "The play was only passable, with or without the four-letter words," Anna said. "His poems are trés lyrical! Trés sensitive!"

The night Ted Fox sauntered into Frank's Place wearing a faded, olive green corduroy sports jacket and wrinkled chino slacks with black Wellington boots, and drunkenly waved a copy of Emily Dickinson in the air, snarling four-letter words for a small band of his admirers, Sis felt an overwhelming desire, she'd never felt before.

At the end of the evening Ted accepted Sis's offer to drive him home. A side trip to the Lovejoy Monument ended in a wrestling match under the watchful eyes of its marble angel. Even the Kotex that revealed that Sis was having her period failed to daunt Ted's lust. Ted wooed Sis and groped her until her blouse was open.

"You're like that angel," he said, pointing up to distract her as he placed his other hand on her bosom. "Your breasts are milk white in the moonlight."

Sis, whose whole concept of love was straight from the romantic movies of the 1950s, felt like she had finally found her hero, but she pushed his hand away and hastily buttoned the blue silk.

Two nights later Ted took Sis to a bar that was in The Regis, a downtown hotel across the street from the Alton Evening Telegraph Building. The lady bartender served Sis without checking to see if she was of legal age, though she was.

After two beers that she did not enjoy but drank because he wanted her to, Sis was willing to park with Ted off Memorial Hospital Drive, even get in the back seat, but when he pushed her to "go all the way," she remembered her father yelling at her. "Boy crazy, you'll end up pregnant like your mother."

She imagined Joe Wasilec Sr., his face bloated with anger, floating there over Ted's right shoulder, yelling at her just like he'd done when she was sixteen and kissed that Italian boy whose father worked with him at the Glass Works.

As Ted lay on her, rubbing between her thighs with one hand and squeezing her breasts with the other, Sis felt herself sinking under his control, but she was able to ask him to stop. After some cajoling, he did stop.

Ted did not call her for three long days. When he did call, he asked her over to his house for lunch and to listen to some great music on his *hi-fi*.

"Ted, are you sure this is okay? What will your mother think if she comes home?"

"She won't come home. I told you. She never comes home during the day." he said, opening the door. She doesn't drive. Dad picks her up at 5:30, and they are home promptly at 5:45 PM, without fail. My parents aren't much, but they're punctual."

The living room was so small that a few pieces of furniture took up the whole space with barely any walking room. There was a brown overstuffed couch, one gold overstuffed chair, and a blonde console television. Ted had rigged up his high-fidelity record player speakers on either side of the television. Sitting next to one of the speakers was a two shelf, dark cherry wood bookcase with rounded edges. He was using it as a cabinet for his records. His mother had draped crocheted doilies over the top of the record cabinet, the television, the head rest of the easy chair, and two head rests on the back of the couch.

"The stereo and records are mine. Mom let me put them up here because there's not room downstairs with all my younger brother's football trophies."

Sis tried to envision an evening at home for Ted. The big easy chair, set off to the side authoritatively, looked like it must be his father's. The two crocheted doilies marked places at either end of the couch. Yet, there were four in the family. Then she noticed a door to a small kitchen off the side of the room. Just inside the door was a straight-backed chair and a sewing cabinet table. Sis intuitively knew that Ted's mother sat there to crochet and watch TV.

Ted motioned for Sis to sit down on the floor in front of the couch. With her feet stretched out, her toes nearly touched the television set.

"We'll get the whole effect of the records this way. I can't believe you haven't ever heard any classical music. What do your folks play?"

"Nothing, really. I have lots of Frank Sinatra records. I'm not into the Beatles or Elvis, the real popular stuff. I do like Bobby Darin's 'Mack the Knife.'"

"You like 'Mack the Knife'? I've got the opera that song's in." He was putting a stack of long-playing records on the spindle.

"I thought we were going to talk about Saturday night," her eyes lowered. "I'm really sorry about what happened. I'd had too much to drink, or I wouldn't have let it go so far. I knew you were mad."

"That was Saturday, we're here now. We'll talk later." Ted handed Sis a can of Pabst Blue Ribbon beer and settled down beside her with his arm behind her on the sofa. "Let's listen to this. See if you recognize your song."

The music of Three Penny Opera was discordant, but Sis listened to the words carefully and began to like the strange new sounds. She also liked being with Ted, close to him, smelling his Old Spice shaving cream, feeling the touch of his arm against hers. He leaned his head slightly to his left and rested it ever so lightly against Sis's cheek. The beer was beginning to relax her. She started to make a comment, but he shushed her.

Ted's arm was resting across her shoulder now, though he was not holding her. Soon his fingers were playing with her collar, and then moving assuredly under her blouse. Sis tried not to stiffen up when she felt his touch. *What could happen here?* she thought. *We're not in the back seat of the car, we're in his living room. He didn't even shut the blinds. It's broad daylight. People can see in from the sidewalk.*

Sis tried to think of something else, anything else. She focused on the music. She tried to listen to the words as she didn't want to miss hearing "Mack the Knife."

Ted was kissing the back of her neck. She could feel his excitement, she was trembling. She wondered if the next record would be the piano concerto Ted had promised to play for her when he invited her over to his house.

"Is the piano music next?"

"Rachmaninoff. Yes. Let's go get something to eat before we listen to it." Ted said, getting up and stopping the record. "There's a market down at the corner."

"I'm not really hungry."

"You will be when you see Mrs. Norton's homemade brownies."

At the one-room corner market where Ted and Sis bought brownies, bologna, and more beer, a neon "Liquor" sign hung over the door and another neon sign in the window announced "Guns and Ammo."

What would Dad say if he saw that? she thought, smiling.

• • •

Sis looked out the window beside her at the tops of the trees and the sky. The sky was a bright fresh blue that afternoon. She heard the train whistle and the clank and creak of the railroad cars moving slowly along the tracks in the valley below State Street. The temperature was hot, eighty-five degrees Fahrenheit, but this downstairs room was cool.

"Are you all right?" Ted asked, sitting up on the side of the bed, half turned toward her, half looking away.

"Uh. Uh huh." She was beginning to shiver as the perspiration dried on her bare skin. The wet sheet beneath her was cold. She wished Ted slept with covers, but the bed only had sheets, and they had been lying on the top sheet.

"Do you want to take a shower? There's one down here." He was sitting straight up now, his back turned to her.

"Yes, I would like that."

"Want to take one together?"

"No."

"Okay, you go first?"

Sis sat up and moved over behind him. On her knees, she ran her hands down Ted's back, felt the soft fine back hair, stared incredulously at the slight curve of his hips.

"Feels good, but this would feel better." He took her hand and started moving it around in front of him. She jerked it back, though part of her wanted to lean forward into him, not resist.

He turned toward her. "You can touch me," he said. "Nothing horrible is going happen. Don't shut your eyes. Look at me."

At first she looked at the top of his head, at his hair—thick, auburn, half-soaked with perspiration. She touched his hair; it was baby fine, too. Then she looked at the naked male body before her. *My god*, she thought. *Boots was right. I do love the feel of him.*

He was kissing her. She shut her eyes again. He was gentler than he had been earlier, and easy to respond to. He was kissing her closed eyes, her cheeks, her neck, her shoulders. Her fears melted away in the heat of his touch. She felt alive and free.

Days later, in the shower, wrapped in the innocent scent of Ivory soap, Ted joyously lathered Sis's now familiar body. He grinned as he broke the bar of soap and handed her half.

The two weeks until Sis left for the University of Illinois passed far too quickly for her. Before she knew it, she was driving the well-worn route between her house and Ted's to say goodbye. He met her at the car, not giving her a chance to get out. He didn't seem to want her to go into the house. He had a package wrapped in grocery bag paper. He just handed it to her through the car window.

"What's this?"

"A present, a going away to school present."

"I thought you never gave presents."

"I don't."

"It looks like records."

"That's probably because it is, something to keep you listening to classical, something to remember me by."

"I could never forget you. Let me come in and open them."

"No, you have to go."

"I don't want to go. I want to stay here with you and Anna, and Mom, and my little brother, Benny. I'm really kind of scared, Ted."

"You're gonna be fine. Besides, what do you mean stay here with me? How long do you think a thing like this lasts? You knew this wasn't going to go on beyond summer vacation. We talked about it that first day."

"I think I love you." Sis said.

"This wasn't love," he said.

"What was it?"

"The last two weeks of summer."

Sis's eyes began to water. "I'm not ready to go."

"No one ever thinks they're ready. But most of the time we are."

"What does that mean?" she asked, a trace of anger rising at his too cool answers.

"I don't know. Just talk. Remember, I'm a wordsmith. Besides, look how ready you were to meet me."

"Braggart!" she said, smiling again.

"Say goodbye. My folks will be back soon. I wouldn't want them to find out now, after it's all over."

"That sounds so matter of fact."

"Well, it is." He started to turn away.

"Kiss me goodbye."

Ted leaned in through the open window and gave Sis a quick kiss on the cheek. She ran her hand through his hair one last time, trying to capture the clean, baby fine feel, wanting to remember it for the times ahead without him.

Walking away, he turned back again. "Hey, don't let those Illinois guys, those fast-talking college boys, bowl you over. You don't want to be easy. You'll lose your self-respect."

"God, Ted. What an awful thing to say."

"I don't mean you were easy. I just don't want you to start believing everything a guy tells you. Some of those frat boys will tell a girl anything just to get her to bed. They'll even tell you they love you."

"That's obviously not necessary, is it? You didn't say you loved me."

"Just the same. Not everybody lets you know where you really stand like I did."

"You might think you cared."

"No, not that! But, who knows? You're going to have Christmas vacation and spring break. I'm just protecting my interests, in case I happen to be around."

• • •

There was a Christmas vacation, and then a tumultuous, on again, off again, four year relationship with Ted that led Sis straight into Harry's possessive arms. Two children and eleven years later, Sis divorced Harry on the grounds of irreconcilable differences.

After Sis's divorce from Harry, she sent Ted the first birthday card. Several years and relationships later, Sis was still struggling with her compulsion to write Ted Fox, wondering why she could not write him what she was really thinking the way she did Aunt Boots or her children, Don and Megan.

When she wrote Ted, the editor in her overshadowed her first instincts.

"Did I tell you that my son Don has decided to come back to Columbia to finish his degree? He won't live at home, but he'll be dropping in a lot. I love the idea of his being in town, but it will add some complications to my love life. As if there aren't enough already."

No, I'll cross out "love-life" and put in "social life."

I think I'll cross out the next line too, "As if there aren't enough already."

I can't believe I haven't finished this letter. I'll have to re-write the whole thing. This is taking revision to obsession. I can't deny it anymore. I am obsessed with Ted Fox lately. I think about him all the time. I even talked to Anna about him at lunch the other day. And I know how much she wants me to forget about that whole time.

"I've been thinking about Alton, and Ted, a lot lately." Sis told Anna. "Remember the time we all got drunk on Thunderbird wine and climbed over the retaining wall at Riverview Park to see the Mississippi better."

Sis was talking as if this was one of her happiest memories. "You and the others stayed close to the wall, but Ted, Arthur, and I sat down and scooted as close to the edge of the bluff as we could get."

"Sure," Anna said. "And I remember that a couple of years later Arthur got high out there on the bluff and thought he could fly to the river. The Telegraph said that the one-hundred-foot fall broke every bone in his body. He was so mangled, they had a closed casket at the funeral."

"I try to think of the good times, not the worst," Sis said.

"Jesus, Mary, and Joseph, Sis, what good times? Ted had you so screwed up you even gave up your baby."

"I asked you never to mention that."

Anna's classic Northern Italian face was cemented in a stern, disapproving frown. Though an artist, Anna was never Bohemian. Her rules for living, handed down from her parents, immigrants from northern Italy, were based on logic and a keen sense of survival.

"What in the hell is going on with you? Telling me fairy tales about how great life with Ted was. And writing him."

"A yearly birthday card and letter, what harm?"

"I can't believe you're writing him at all!" Anna said, giving her latte a fierce stir. "He's part of the past."

"You're part of that past, too," Sis said. "And I haven't stopped caring about you."

"Ted's a part of your past that's best left there." Anna's final comment was, "You should put everything about Ted Fox out of your mind once and for all and get on with your life."

After seeing Anna, Sis kept busy, forcing herself to stop thinking about Ted, partially because of her own good sense, but also out of deference to her friend's advice. Still, she couldn't control her unconscious, and night after night she was startled out of sleep by dreams of Ted.

Not the kind of dreams Sis had about Ted when she was first married to Harry, the ones where Ted was chasing Harry and her in a rage, waving a gun and yelling that he'd kill her before he'd let her marry Harry Jenkins. In those dreams, just as Ted was about to catch her, he'd stop dead still and look at her with the wiseacre grin she had learned to love in the good times and say, "Come on, baby, you can't tell me you'd rather have happiness with him than excitement with me?"

She would wake up screaming and, if Harry woke up, she would tell him that she was having a nightmare about water bugs crawling all over the walls.

Sis's dreams this summer and fall did not leave her in fear for her life, but they were disturbing. One night she woke up in a cold sweat dreaming that Ted was there. Waking, she wrote in her journal, "I could feel the warmth of his body against mine as he kissed me. When I woke up, I was terrified, afraid that he was kissing me goodbye. I had to sit up and turn on a light to get my head together, to remember where I was and who I am now." Ted and Sis had kissed goodbye nearly thirty years before.

Shadows covered the plants on the sill with dark blotches, and the evening light was no longer strong enough to write. The dog was restlessly tugging at the leg of Sis's sweatpants, anxious to go out for their daily walk.

"Not now, Mutt, I've still got to finish this damned birthday letter to Ted."

She got up and stretched her arms and legs as she walked over to switch on the overhead light. Writing Ted's letter had taken up a whole beautiful day when she could have been working in the garden, taking Mutt for a really long afternoon walk, or sitting in her special spot, high up on a ledge above Rock Quarry Road. From there, if the limbs were nearly bare, like now, she could see the rooftops of the town across the creek, stretching away to the west.

Evening was upon her, and Sis had not written her weekly letters to her grown children, Don and Megan, who both lived out of state, or to Aunt Boots who was still going strong in a small home in Alton.

Moreover, this day's memories were not just the selectively good memories of Ted that she had kept at the front of her mind for all these years. *Have I really forgotten and forgiven all the pain? Between Dad, Ted, and Harry, I've certainly had enough. Did I just whitewash it like Mom used to?*

Sis had always been introspective—some felt to her detriment, but she was proud that she did as much as she could to understand herself. Megan was like her in that, and Don, too. But Sis thought she might be making too much of this. Why was sending birthday cards to Ted any more meaningful than sending cards to other old friends? She knew the answer. Because she didn't spend whole days writing and rewriting letters to her other old friends.

After her marriage to Harry ended, there were several lovers, all properly hidden from the children until they were old enough to understand. But none had lasted. Sis thought of this now.

I don't want to give Ted even a hint of how much loving him, knowing that I could love someone longer than six years, six months, or six days means to me. God, what if someday he signs a letter, "Love, as always, Ted." I'd never be free!

Sis grabbed up all the pages of the letter to Ted and started ripping them into shreds. When she was finished, she looked down at the scattered balls of crunched up drafts on the floor and then at the pile of confetti in the middle of her kitchen table, shocked at the mess it made.

A corner of the birthday card was sticking out from under the mess on the table. Sis picked it up and looked at it again. It was a great card! Ted would really like it.

Sis had signed it earlier, after much thought, of course, not with love, or as always, or fondly, but "Peace, love, and joy, Sis," a general-use signature. Now she slipped the card back into its already stamped and addressed envelope, gathered up a handful of the torn remains of letter, and started to pitch it all into the wastepaper basket.

What a waste, she thought. *Fifty is an important birthday. He's going to feel old. This might turn the day around for him. I didn't say anything damning. What harm can one birthday card do?*

Sis thought of all the fruitless years of cards, letters, and answers. *A lot!* With deliberate finality, Sis deposited the card and the remains of her last letter to Ted into the trash.

Solitaire
Columbia, MO — 1990s

Today is mine. I am not going to spend this morning waiting for Edmund to call. I will take a hot bubble bath and let the water drain down to nothing while I sit in the tub reading and drying off. The way my body feels while I'm air drying is as refreshing and relaxing as the fragile soap bubbles popping on my skin while I bathe.

I leave the bathroom door open so I'm not totally cut off from the house. Occasional companionable sounds reach me in my warm sanctuary. I hear the gentle splash of water rippling through the air filter on my aquarium and the steady, soft chatter of the grandfather clock.

When I get out of the tub, the bottoms of my feet, the back of my heels, a bit of my backside, and the crevices under my arms and breasts are still wet. The scent of lavender bath oil hangs in the air.

Though Edmund's arrival interrupted my bath, this Saturday morning is especially sweet because I didn't expect to see him. After we make love, he holds me more tightly than usual and strokes my shoulders and back. I enjoy the stroking and the sharp, acrid smell of his sweat.

He does not ask me how things are going at the bookstore I manage, although he'll listen if I say I have a problem I want to talk to him about. He especially likes to give me advice about budgeting my money or fixing my car. But he never asks me about anything. He just starts in talking about his life. That's all right. I love to listen to him talk. His voice has a sexy quality. I think that's what first attracted me to him, his voice and his jolly, waggish eyes.

With him, I'm not just a solitary, fifty-four-year-old empty nester. I'm content again. Content to lie beside him and hear his voice. Content to hear him tell me all about his other life, his real life.

His daughter is on his mind today, and his voice is sad. "Nancy came over for dinner last night and dropped a real bomb on us. She's pregnant."

"Is she going to keep the baby?"

"Of course not. She'll have an abortion. We've already made the appointment."

"How does she feel about that?" I ask. "How does your wife feel?"

"How can they feel? She's still in graduate school. She knows what she has to do." His voice is both angry and sad now. "It's hard enough for her, going to school, working. And the guy who got her pregnant is ignoring her. He's no support at all."

• • •

Lying beside Edmund, I am light years away in terms of my life. I'm in St. Louis, Missouri, thirty-five years ago, and I feel the bitter cold of that winter. Ted Fox is beside me in bed, second-hand covers heaped over us. I can see his breath as he talks. I can't get warm.

"If you're pregnant, we'll deal with it," he reassures me and pulls me closer to him. "Come on, Honey. I didn't drive all the way back tonight to talk. I just spent three days at home with my folks. I need comfort."

Why can't I ever say no to Ted? Why can't I ask him for comfort? Or get mad and just hop up out of bed and tell him to fuck off. Tell him that three days with his mother and father hardly compares to thinking you're pregnant. How in the hell does that compare to a streetcar trip across town in the dead of winter to a home for unwed mothers? How in the hell does three days with his family compare to waiting in that sterile room, wondering what to say to the stranger walking in.

"I think I'm pregnant and there's no way I can keep the baby."

I roll over on my side with my back to him, and he sidles up to me. "My god, she made me eat pancakes and eggs and bacon for three days," he complains. "One morning I even yelled at her. 'God dammit, mother, I don't want your fucking eggs.' But she pretended not to hear me."

Why can't I yell at him, the way he yelled at her? "God dammit, Ted, I don't want to hear about your fucking mother." Isn't being pregnant as important as having to eat pancakes? "God dammit, Ted, do you know what it's like to think you may have life inside you and know that all you can do with it is kill it or give it away?" And worse, to know that the father is so screwed up on drugs that you wouldn't marry him if he asked you.

What had the lady at the home said? She had been kind, tried to comfort me. "Don't worry." She knew that I could get away with going out of town for a few months. I wouldn't have to tell my mother. I had explained that I was sure this would kill her. Mother had never been able to cope with anything sexual.

I don't even know how mother managed to get pregnant with me. When I asked her about sex, how it felt, she said, "I can't remember ever enjoying it." Maybe that's why my father left us.

The lady at the home said they had managed situations like this before. I could say I was going away to train for a new job. They would send me a letter on some official letterhead. They would find a good home for the baby. The last thing she said to me was, "This will work out; everything will be all right."

"How do I know it's mine?" Ted's eyes had that steel-cold look he got when he wanted his way. It was a look that scared me. "How do I know you didn't sleep with Jack Hawkins the weekend I was in Boston? Everybody knows he stayed here on his way to Canada. I know you sleep with all my friends."

"What you know is that all your friends hit on me!" I shouted. "You know that because you know what bastards they are. They think I'm easy because we live together. I don't sleep with them."

"How do I know you're pregnant anyway?"

I sigh.

He holds me close. I can't remember the last time he really held me close. "Let's talk about this in the morning. I want you now."

After Ted finished, he rolled over away from me and said, "Get some sleep. We'll work things out tomorrow."

The last thing he said to me was, "Don't worry, everything will turn out all right."

In the morning, right after Ted woke up and had sex with me again, he moved out of my apartment and into Marvin and Janet's. He didn't wait until after breakfast to do it. I'm not even sure he washed.

He just gathered his records, his books, a couple of my books, and his shaving kit, and moved next door.

• • •

I lie here thinking about a baby girl I saw just once, Ted's and mine. In my mind, I named her Thea, after Ted. She had the softest reddish-gold, baby fuzz hair. Her fingers were long and thin. She could be a basketball player or a concert pianist. Even now, I can imagine her playing Rachmaninoff or Mozart for me.

• • •

I feel a familiar hardness touching my bare stomach and raise my eyes to his face. For a brief instant, I expect to see Ted.

Edmund, his soft gray hair still damp with sweat, is talking about his daughter again. "She's so alone. Even though we're there, she's so alone."

This man who went from his mother's home to his wife's arms and hasn't slept alone in forty years is talking about being alone as if he understood. This man—who goes from his wife's arms to mine and back again. I shut my eyes—try to let the feel, sound, and smell of him make me happy for a while longer. I wonder if he will never know how alone a person can be.

Her Mother's Daughter
Iowa City, IA — circa 1996

Until gardening took over my life, I struggled to figure out what I was going to do with it. Like many other twenty-somethings in Iowa City, Iowa, the Peace Corps returnees "Center of the World," I was caught in a flood of college graduates who couldn't find decent jobs. I thought of making and selling all-natural lotions or giving up any thought of a rewarding career and becoming a couch potato, while Andrew, my partner, supported us. I had the option of pursuing a new field in graduate school, one that MIGHT have a possibility of resulting in gainful employment. My friend Lucy and I were in much the same situation when we learned that for a small amount of rent, we could have our own plot in Troy Community Gardens. We went for it.

Everything in our garden grew well except the pea plants. We mourned the loss of the pea plants as if they were our progeny and turned to our neighbors who worked the surrounding garden plots for comfort. I mentioned our problem to an older Asian woman who directed a sizeable mixed group of Asian gardeners.

"Our peas died," I said. "Everything else lived."

"Peas planted too late," she said. Then we heard her disdainful answer ripple across the waves of vegetables. "Planted too late," a chant said over and over in various Asian accents.

When my mother visited last summer, she found it hard to comprehend that after all the years she unsuccessfully begged me to help in her flower gardens, I would choose to have a garden, or that I could be a really good gardener, even with Lucy's help.

"When you told me you had a garden, you didn't say it was a small truck farm," Mother's eyes opened wide to give her an awestruck expression I knew from our many trips and family adventures. No matter how many cities we saw, or Victorian houses with lacework wooden balconies and velvet-wall-papered rooms we visited, my mother's natural child would burst onto the scene and take everything in with enthusiasm.

"It's an ordinary plot," I said, downplaying her enthusiasm, as I often do, though I don't know why.

The old Hmong woman in the next plot noticed my mother inspecting the burned-out peas, looked up from her stooped position picking beans, and began the chant, "Planted too late."

"When did you plant the peas?" Mother asked.

"When everyone else did."

"Well, apparently not when everyone else did," my mother said. "Theirs lived."

The muscles in my throat tightened. I was afraid that if I spoke, I would scream. But unaware of the effect her comment had on me, Mom was bending down again, examining the complex intertwining of the bean plants with obvious admiration.

"Look at these green beans! You're going to have to take a stand at the farmer's market to get rid of them," she said, excited.

Even though her excitement was genuine, it was wearing. I looked at her, bending down in the bean patch, helping me pick, putting the beans into the fishnet bag I gave her, fussing with the one's that stuck out through the netting, trying to push them in, only to find that others worked their way out in another spot. The broad expanse of her backside in a brightly patterned split skirt reminded me of wooden grandmas bent over in suburban yards, with their white lace pantaloons showing under flour sack skirts.

"These will be wonderful steamed." Mother stood up, proudly showing me a handful of my own beans. "Will you fix some for supper tonight?"

"I thought you were going to take us out tonight."

"Oh, yes, I forgot. Could we do it tomorrow?"

"No, we can't do it tomorrow, Mom. I told Andrew we'd meet him in town tonight," I said.

"I meant the steaming, you misunderstood," she said.

"You didn't try to change plans just now? Of course not, I'm always the one who is wrong."

"Not always, but maybe this time. It's such a little thing to fuss about."

"Mom, it doesn't matter when you're home alone, but when Andrew and I commit to do something, we do it." All the while, I was picking up the tools and bags of vegetables. I started toward the edge of the garden patch, still talking. "I just wish you wouldn't change your mind all the time," I said, turning my head to face her.

"I didn't change my mind. Dammit, I forgot." Her face was flushing.

I acted as if I didn't hear her, the way Henry our terrier does, when he's trotting down the road just outside her reach. *You think you're so wonderfully flexible*, I thought, *but you're really flighty. Indecisive.*

When we were in the car, I turned to her, "Mom, you don't realize it but changing your mind all the time makes it hard on everyone else.

My mother loved to take day or weekend trips with us. My older brother, Don, and I had a chance to see many places and things other kids never even imagined. But we never knew whether or not we would end up where our mother said we were going or doing what she said we were going to do. We might head for St. Louis and end up at Hermann because she saw a sign for the Mai Fest.

"Remember that time we were going to the lake," I said, still holding the keys in the ignition.

"I took you to the lake several times every summer. Which one?"

"The time when we were halfway there, and you decided that we'd been to the lake a lot that summer so it might be more fun for us to see the river below the dam. Of course, the river's current was too fast for you to let us sit on the bank and fish, which is what we really wanted to do, and we could have done it at the lake."

"But we got to see that fishing boat floating down the river by itself with two men in another boat trying to catch it. You talked about it for days."

"That doesn't mean that you can just change plans for everyone whenever you want."

"Can we go home now?" she said with a sigh. "I have to pee."

"You always have to pee when I'm finally telling you something important."

"Okay but you can explain to Andrew if I pee in his car." Her mouth had that squinched look, the one she gets just before she cries.

I started the car up, feeling like I was one of the paper butterflies she hangs on a string over the kitchen table, swinging in one direction when the window by the sink is open and another if the back door is ajar.

"You don't know how many times you embarrassed me in front of my friends, Mom. Like that time you wouldn't let me go rappelling after I'd made all the plans." This was argument number 3A. I brought it up whenever I could because I believed someday she would admit she was wrong.

The car was turning the corner. I was driving home without thinking, engrossed in getting her to admit her culpability, but she gave me the same weary answer.

"For God's sake, Megan, all the parents were worried. We didn't know the instructor's qualifications. I had to say 'No.'"

"Do you always have to be right?" I said.

"According to you, I'm never right." The slick drops of tears that had piled up behind my mother's eyelids slid over onto her cheeks.

I felt cruel, worthless, ungrateful, but I wondered if she broke into tears when she disagreed with one of the ladies in her bi-weekly dinner group, a colleague at the office, one of her students, my brother Don, or if it was just with me. Every time we were alone together for more than a few hours, this happened. I think of us like two different weather fronts. You put us in the same space, and you get storms.

When she had control of her voice, she said. "Let's not fight, honey. We've been doing so well this trip."

How could she think we were doing well? I was enjoying her visit so much that I couldn't wait for the next morning when I could go back to a temp job I hated.

She reached over and patted my leg. "I was trying to show you how proud I am of you and your garden."

Andrew and Mom think a pat, a hug, or any physical expression of love will resolve all problems.

"Can we drop it?" I said in a tone that warned her not to touch me again.

"Okay." She said and was quiet.

The rest of the way home, the loud snap of crisp beans breaking resounded in the silence of the car.

• • •

I love my mother as much as anyone loves their mother. But that's part of the problem. I feel like I should love her more somehow. When I was in high school all my friends wanted to have a mother they could talk to like I talked to mine, a mother that respected them and treated them like grown-ups. But now, whenever I'm with her, she treats me like a child, and then I behave like a child. I hate myself for hurting her. She hates herself for hurting me. I hate myself for making her hate herself. It's an impossible cycle of sadness. No matter how I work to prepare myself for being with her, this always happens.

I have begun to doubt all the good memories my friends and I have of this woman. How can the two people be one? Sometimes I think I must have made it all up, the way she makes up the guys she goes out with. Whenever she tells me about a new guy, I know exactly what she's going to say about him. Even though they're all quite different, she describes the same guy, the one she wants them to be. When they turn out to be something else, she says she never should have trusted them.

• • •

"Mom, I yelled from the back door. "It's that jerk, Edmund, again. One ring!"

Mom dropped her trowel in the new iris bed and came springing up the back hill like a young animal. Her reddish-blonde hair glistened in the sun, and her breasts bounced inside the loose-fitting T-shirt with the "Save the Whales" slogan. She dialed the number, and it was only seconds before he answered. "Sure. Half an hour," she said and hung up. "Honey, you don't mind if I go into town for an hour or so to meet Edmund, do you? You and I can go to the 4:30 movie."

"Why ask?" I said. "You've already told him you'd come."

"I could call back and tell him I can't."

"He's such a jerk, Mom, calling you and ringing once, expecting you to come running whenever he wants you."

"You know he's married. It's difficult for him to plan ahead. Lots of times I can't go when he calls."

"Yeah, when?"

"When I have to work. When we have something planned that can't be changed."

"Go on, Mom," I said. "I'm going to go over to Dad's and help him paint his picnic table this morning anyway."

She heard the disdain in my voice. "Why do you dislike Edmund so?" she asked. "You don't even know him."

"Because you deserve better. A man who respects you. What have you always told me, 'Make boys respect me.'"

"This is different. It's not a matter of respect. You'll understand someday."

"I understand now, Mom. Believe me, I do."

"Perhaps, I shouldn't have told you and Don that he was married, but I don't like to lie to you."

My mother has a "thing" about lying. From what she says, Grandma Helen was always telling what she called "white lies." Mom never knew what was true and what was a white lie that Grandma made up to make things seem better.

"Never mind, Mom. Go see Edmund."

"You pick out the movie you want to see. I'll be home by two, have the garden weeded by 3:30, and we can get there in plenty of time. Do you want to go to House of Chow after? This is turning out to be a great weekend," she said.

I watched her rush into the bathroom to take a spit bath, as she called it, and then throw on a light summer dress, hurry to the car, and leave. It all took a matter of minutes. He called, she went.

• • •

The five months this spring that I've been living at home, taking care of my mother's house and gardens came about unexpectedly, but not inexplicably. By Thanksgiving last year, Andrew and I were having serious problems, but neither one of us wanted to admit it. He had a great, high paying job he loved and no college degree. I had a degree from a highly respected eastern university and a low paying temp job, I hated.

This bothered both of us in different ways. Even though we prorated the expenses based on our incomes, I felt dependent. He felt pressured to go back to college, and he was. His family and I continually pressed him to finish his degree, fearful that someday he'd regret not getting it. Both our families thought we each were holding the other back.

At Christmas, Andrew went to his parents' house, and I went to be with my family. My mother was doing desktop publishing from my childhood home. Her business had started to mushroom, and she asked me if I wanted to come into it with her.

"I need the help, and you are a great editor," she said. "Take a break from Andrew. It'll do you both good."

My mother has radar when it comes to romantic trouble.

"No!" I said. "Absolutely no way, Mom."

By February when she asked me again, Andrew and I were arguing at least three times a week over something—money, my going back to school, his going back to school, our future in general, and whether or not we had one.

• • •

"Why don't you quit that temp job you hate so much and just stay home?" Andrew yelled above the sound of the sports announcer on the TV. He hardly ever raised his voice, even when he was his most angry, he usually just brooded. That night, during two hours of ESPN commercial breaks, we had been "discussing" my record-breaking-deplorable job.

"And what if I go another six months or a year before I find a real job?"

"We can make it on my salary," Andrew said. "You could take watercolor lessons again and sell your paintings at the art fairs. Paint all winter, sell all summer."

"Then your parents could really say that I'm what's keeping you from going back to school!"

"We could get married. My folks wouldn't be so difficult if there were grandchildren in the future."

"I don't want to get married until we're both out of debt."

"So, you never want to get married," Andrew said, smiling, perhaps hoping I'd give it a break.

"It's not funny. No matter how hard things got, Mom never took any money from her men, unless it was her birthday or something."

"Oh, yes! You told me her stance on that! What makes you think she's right?"

"I happen to agree with her."

He began to imitate my mom on her soap box, "If you take money from a man, no matter how much you love each other, you'll get dependent on him; and if it goes bad, you won't be able to get free." Andrew, the mimic, had her gestures and tone of voice down pat, and I had given him the quotes, myself.

"Stop making fun of my Mom!"

"The one who drives you crazy!"

"If we can't have a simple discussion without bringing my mother into it, how could you ever expect us to have a decent marriage?"

"What?"

"You heard me." I was on the couch, my head in my hands, about to cry. I never want to cry in an argument. I'm stronger than she is.

Andrew slid over closer and started to put his arm around me.

"Don't," I said, moving away. "When is this damned basketball game going to be over?"

"Let's turn it off and go to bed."

"Now you want to turn it off and go to bed. Watch your game. I'm going to the kitchen to read."

• • •

I didn't join my mom in her business. I am smart enough to steer clear of that. But, my Aunt Boots, who has been a surrogate grandmother to Don and me, is in her eighties. In late February, she got too ill to be left alone and my mother called to suggest the arrangement that brought me home. Mother would live with Aunt Boots in Alton, Illinois, 135 miles away from my mid-Missouri hometown by the interstate, and I would live at the homestead, caring for the gardens and the pets. By then, my mother's one patch of third-generation family irises had grown to several smaller groupings in the front yard, plus peonies, jonquils and daffodils, roses, and in the back yard, a butterfly garden, more irises, and a shade garden.

Before I gave in, I tried to dissuade her. "Why don't you rent the house out, get a little extra income?" I said.

"Have strangers living in it? And what about Henry and Mia?" My mother gives her dog and cat human names, no Spots or Snowballs for her. "Besides, I'd have to guarantee renters a certain amount of time in the place. What if I needed it back before the renter's lease was up."

Mom is really saying that Aunt Boots might die soon, and I feel a twinge of anxiety. Aunt Boots could die before I've heard all her stories about the family, about my Mom, and it would all be gone forever. I don't trust my mom's stories that much anymore.

A week later I agree to the arrangement, sadly realizing that I might miss Lucy and the cats more than I miss Andrew. I hope this is not a foreshadowing that I will end my life without a significant male other the way so many of the women in my family have. I pack just what I need for the spring and summer and leave Andrew on his own for the duration, except for our cats, Jake and Harry.

Nurturing the flowers, I am aware of myself as a member of a special club, generations of women in my family whose main pleasure in life was their flowers. I begin to think that if I knew those women better, I might know myself better and be able to find my focus. My hands in the soil, bringing fragrance and color to my mother's yard, are my true connection to an extended family, something that has always been disjointed for me because I cannot remember what life was like before my parents were divorced.

I want to know all about my mom's family, all about Mom and Dad when they were married, as much of the history of my life as I can. When Brad Denton, our neighbor across the street whom I had always called Uncle Brad, comes over and admires the work I have done with the irises, I say, "Uncle Brad, how long did you know Mom and Dad before the divorce?"

"A couple years, I guess," he says.

"What were they like?" I ask.

"Other couples. They seemed to get along when Marian and I were around. Marian says they didn't, that I'm just too insensitive to notice."

"Is Marian coming back soon?" I ask. I know she is in Ohio at her folks.

"I don't know. She and the kids are having a great time in Cleveland, if you can believe that," he says, grinning. "I miss them a hell of a lot," he says. "We used to take our bikes on the Katy Trail every Sunday this time of year. I haven't gone once since they've been away."

I look at him more closely at that moment. The thick bull neck, the massive shoulders, the weathered tan from working in the sun, and the lazy, playful look in his eyes are completely different from Andrew's long slim neck and body, his pale, studied professional look, his fashionable clothes, and his techno-aesthetic look.

I must look sympathetic because the next thing he says is, "Hey, would you like to take a bike ride with me some weekend?"

I don't know what to say, and after a while, I say, "Sure. As long as I'm here, I might as well enjoy the advantages of the area."

Now, Brad and I ride bikes every weekend that Mom isn't home, or I'm not in Illinois. It's amazing how much we have in common, though he is nine years older and married with children. We often go to Les Bourgeois Winery after our rides, and people there think of us as a couple. We play it to the hilt in front of strangers, no harm done because I have been absolutely firm. On the occasional times Brad does try to make a move, I make it clear that all I want is a friendship. I have a partner I love. I also know Brad would not be the least interested in me if he weren't missing Marian so much. I am confident of that.

Tending my mother's flowers is surprisingly different from working with our vegetable garden. Specific things are the same, weeding and watering top that list, but with a flower garden you are not obligated to pick the flowers. You pick them for bouquets, or to float in a brandy snifter, or to place one perfect bud in a vase and watch it bloom, but you don't feel the pressure to pick flowers that you do to pick tomatoes, beans, zucchinis, cucumbers, peppers, and lettuce.

Last summer, the vegetables, the picking and preparing, not to mention consuming, became all important. I lived that whole summer by a singular, personal rule. If I were into needle point, I probably would have made a wall decoration with this rule on it. "If you grow them, you've got to pick, clean, snap, peel, preserve, prepare, and eat them."

• • •

"Zucchini soup?" Andrew is standing by the small apartment stove. "Good, God. How many ways are we going to have to eat zucchini?"

"I don't know," I say, wiping my forehead with the food stained, flour smudged apron I'm wearing. He has not changed clothes for dinner, and I enjoy looking at his long lean body, in the fashionable dress clothes he always wears to work. "There are still quite a few recipes I haven't tried."

"Could you save them for next year's crop? Cook something else for a while. Let ME cook something else."

"We're having spaghetti squash with marinara, and my special low-cost Caesar salad tomorrow night when Lucy's here."

"Great, I'll pick up some Italian bread at Gino's," Andrew says.

"Don't have to."

"I want to."

"You'll spoil the surprise."

"What surprise?" he says, turning to go back to the six o'clock sports news. As much as I hate being a sports widow, I always view Andrew being a sports nut as another sure sign that he is totally different from the kind of men Mom went with. She made a policy of never going out with any man who was hung up on sports. Horses, yes. Politics, yes. Art, yes. But not sports.

"The surprise Lucy has for you," I say.

"Let me guess, she's making some kind of Italian bread out of zucchini and mozzarella."

"She told you?" I say and continue to stir.

• • •

Flower gardens don't give you that kind of guilt, even if they are your mother's. They bloom better if you pick them regularly, but taking care of irises and daffodils in the spring can be as effortless as sitting on the porch swing or a wrought iron bench on the patio, enjoying their beauty. You simply cannot pull up a chair by the vegetable garden and relax, read a book, or drink your morning coffee. I was always a hot tea and milk person, but I am beginning to like my mother's Folger's coffee singles.

With a flower garden, even weeding can be neglected for a short time. As long as the ground stays soft, you can leave the encroaching dandelions and grass for a weekend or two while you go to the movies or ride a bike on the Katy trail with your Uncle Brad.

• • •

"That's what makes our marriage so good," Brad says.

We are sitting on a concrete bench at a viewing area on the trail, Brad's hand rests next to mine, barely touching, but I feel it to my toes. The Missouri River is close to us, like the

Osage was the time mother took us below the dam, but she wasn't with me now, thwarting my desire to get closer to the water.

"Marian has her interests and I have mine," Brad says. "We don't have to spend every moment with each other like some of our friends who fight all the time."

"If Andrew and I went our own ways," I say, "I'd never see him except in bed." *My God, that wouldn't be that much different than Edmund and mother*, I think, and jump up from the bench, ready to go. "Beat you to the parking lot," I yell, and we are off and running.

• • •

"Did every woman in the last few generations of our family get a divorce except you, Aunt Boots?" I'm sitting in the small red and white kitchen eating cookies with Aunt Boots while Mom watches a movie on the TV in the living room. Boots's house has four rooms and a bath, the perfect size for a woman alone.

"I was divorced," she says.

"I thought you and Uncle Macon were married thirty-five years before he died," I say.

"Thirty-six."

"So, you were divorced from your first husband, Mae Ellen's dad?"

"Nope, widowed."

"I thought you said you were divorced."

"I was divorced from my second husband. He only lasted three months." Aunt Boots tries to get up from her chair. Her back is bent so badly her chin almost touches her stomach.

"Don't get up," I say. "What do you want? I'll get it."

"A cup of those sugar-free peach halves to go with my cookies."

"You remind me of Morn. She drinks diet Coke but has Ben and Jerry's ice cream every night before she goes to bed."

"Not here she doesn't," Boots says. "It's too expensive. She isn't buying that overpriced crap, is she?"

"Never mind, I'll get your peaches. Tell me about your other husbands."

"Not much to tell. One got shot . . ."

"Was that Mae Ellen's dad?" I ask.

"And your Grandma Helen didn't like the other one."

"Why not?"

"He cheated at cards," she says.

"The one that got shot?"

"No," she says. "Mae Ellen's dad got shot doing something he shouldn't of done."

I want to know more, but Aunt Boots is drifting off, so I put her to bed and cover her with the red and white afghan one of the women in our family crocheted for her. I start to ask her who made the afghan but decide not to. I have to get up early in the morning to drive back to Columbia before the Sunday traffic gets too bad. Besides, Mom and I are getting along this weekend. It is best to go home before we have to talk about anything substantive.

When I get back to Columbia, there is a message from Andrew on the answering machine. "Your vegetable plot is in danger. Call Lucy ASAP."

I call and learn that the acreage that Iowa City used for the community garden really belonged to the state, and the governor's new budget has recommended selling off the property by the end of the year. We would be plotless, Lucy and I, the Hmongs, and the vegetables.

"When did you hear about this?" I ask after I reach Lucy at 1:00 AM.

"Just today. Andrew saw the article in the morning paper and showed it to me at lunch," Lucy says.

"Lunch?"

"Yes, I had some shopping to do downtown, so I met him for lunch. Big deal. I have supper with him almost every night."

"That's different," I say. "You have supper with Andrew and me every night when I'm there. That shouldn't change, but lunch?"

"Megannnn! Helloo! This is your friend talking. Me, Lucy."

"You know, my mother made an insinuation this weekend about how pretty you are and how much you look like me, especially in that one snapshot of you cooking at our place. Mom actually thought you were me."

"So?"

"Anyway, she made this cliché wisecrack about the mice playing . . . you know."

"Megannn! You have to know that all the time Andrew and I are together is spent consoling ourselves over missing you. Even when he comes out to work in the garden."

"Andrew is working in the garden!"

"Well, I can't do it all alone," Lucy says. "Two plots. If I didn't take both plots, we might not get another chance to get two adjoining plots for several years." She stopped to draw a breath. "Maybe never if the governor gets his way. Your mom doesn't know the governor of Iowa, does she?"

I don't remember telling Lucy about Mom and politics. Mother facilitated the annual Governor's Conference on Higher Education for Missouri's Governor Ashcroft, when he was president of the national organization. That was how she made an acquaintance with Dukakis's right-hand man for education. Turned out the guy ended up in jail for something.

My mother had terrible taste in men after the divorce. She would probably say before the divorce, too.

My mother's political adventures were the reason I'd never been very politically inclined. Mom dated a lobbyist for six years after the divorce. He always seemed kind of wishy-washy and insincere, taking whatever side he was told his boss wanted him to. But my grandmother Helen was supposed to have known and worked for Adlai Stevenson during his campaign for Governor of Illinois. That's one of Mom's family legends, like when Mom marched through the worst streets of Chicago in a parade for Jack Kennedy in 1960 and then wasn't even able to see him from the seats that were reserved for the Young Democrats. She said he was just a dark speck on the stage, but she'd never forget his voice.

• • •

I asked Mom once, I think it was right after Andrew and I started living together, why she had married a small-town schoolteacher like my dad when she was so attracted to men with power.

"We shouldn't talk about your dad. It always starts a fight," she said.

"I don't like it when you say bad things about Dad, that's all. He's my dad and I love him."

"I've always tried to encourage you and Don to love your father, you know that." I nodded in assent and then she asked, "Is knowing why I married your dad really important to you?"

"Well, I am curious," I said. "He's not exactly your type."

"I thought I loved him," she said.

Andrew and I discuss this a lot now, trying to figure out how you know the difference between being in love and just thinking you are in love. I worry that we just think we're in love.

My mind back on track, I say, "I'll mention the garden problem to her. Email me the article."

"You and your mom getting along?" Lucy asks.

"Yeah, surprisingly well. And we're not really trying that hard either," I say. "We see each other about every other week. She comes here, or I go there."

"So call her up and ask her if she knows our governor. And if she mentions Andrew and me again, tell her that I'm a lesbian. That'll shut her up."

"She'd just say that you're probably bisexual."

"Megan, you don't realize how lucky you are. My mom won't even say bisexual."

• • •

All the neighbors are beginning to tell me that when I'm working in the garden, they forget it's me and think Mom is home. And Brad constantly tells me how much I remind him of my mother. I am beginning to like being her house-sitter and gardener. I know that someday she will sit with a friend or a grandchild, when my brother and I have children, on the patio she built on her hands and knees, patio stone by patio stone, pointing out the new mock orange bush, commenting that it reminds her of her childhood when she lived in the house on Edwards Street, her bed, a day-bed on the sun porch, and the scent of the mock orange bush spreading into her dreams on warm spring nights when the windows were up. She will say, "My daughter Megan planted that bush for me the spring she was home to help out."

When I look out the back door this morning, the great yellow Prince Albert Jonquils that mother planted to naturalize the back slope are still in bloom. These were my grandmother Helen's favorite flowers, or so my mother says, though she also mentions peace roses, camellias, and irises.

Mother keeps a picture of Grandma Helen on the hutch in the dining room, right next to one of Grandpa Joe.

It's hard for me to think of the woman in the picture as my grandmother. I never knew her. I figured out that I'm two years older now than my mother was when Grandma died. I can't imagine what it would be like if Mom died, as hard as it is to get along with her. Life without her as close as a phone call would be unbearable.

Maybe it's seeing Grandma's picture every day, but I'm beginning to wonder what my grandma was really like. My mother doesn't talk about her much, but when she does, it's like she's talking about a different woman every time.

Yesterday I found an old book, THE IRIS, copyright 1959, written by an Englishman. It made me think about Edmund again. That's probably why Mom bought it, too. It reminded her of Edmund.

This guy was such a jerk, not talking to Don and me on the phone, like we didn't exist. If I answered he would hang up immediately. He told Mom he felt bad about talking to us because he was married.

I was angry at him all the time because he was hurting my mother. I could see it, even if she didn't. She didn't even give other guys a chance. Not to mention that he thought my brother and I were so stupid we couldn't figure out who she was talking to. He didn't care a bit about us not knowing. I think he was just afraid we'd tell someone who would tell someone else and it might get back to his wife.

All those years they were together, and he didn't even know my Morn well enough to know she wouldn't lie to Don and me about who he was. It still makes me angry whenever I think of it.

Mom was always straight with us about anything we asked her. Whatever it was, she would sit down and try to explain it to us. We didn't always understand, but we knew she was telling us the truth. Mom never lied to us, she only lied to herself.

Edmund, the Brit, lasted longer than any of the others, twelve years or so. He wasn't just one of her summer romances. Mom fell in love practically every summer until she met Edmund. He's been gone two years now. Moved to Carolina, or maybe Canada, she won't say. She doesn't seem to want to meet anyone new, but I fully expect her to meet someone in Alton this summer.

• • •

"When the weather's warm, I get amorous." She's telling me this sitting on the patio with a glass of cabernet that Brad bought today when we took Mom to the Shelter Gardens and then went out to see the river from Les Bourgeois Winery. "Didn't Andrew and you fall in love in the summer?"

"We didn't exactly fall, we were friends for six months before our first date," I say. "But it was summer."

"I could never live in California. I'd want to be making love all the time," she says.

"Too much information," I say.

"Better for me to be in Iowa City like you and Andrew," she says.

"Are you trying to tell me something that I am not going to like hearing?"

"No, just a comment. Actually, I always figured that you went to Iowa City and Don went to Maine because you were sure I'd never follow you there."

"Jesus, Mom."

"Talking about summer romances," she says.

"Were we?"

"I have something serious I want to talk to you about," she says.

"You met someone in Alton." I'm all ears, intent on every word.

"I wish."

"I don't want to hear about anything else," I say. "Serious talk could spoil this wonderful day."

"It can't wait," she says.

"Not even for morning?"

"No, I might not have the courage to say this tomorrow."

"Mom, please," I say. "This has been a great day. Don't spoil it."

"I don't want to, but we really have to talk. Remember when I was suspicious of Andrew and Lucy spending so much time together?"

"Sure, I was really pissed." I had been angry, even though I knew Mom, the child of the 60s, did not understand the attitude my friends and our partners, married or unmarried, have toward sex. I try again. "It's not just how we feel about each other, or commitments, we have to be monogamous. Promiscuity is too dangerous these days," I say. Talk about soap boxes. I'm giving Mom an earful.

"I guess you mean AIDS," she says, "and all the crazies out there."

"Well, yes." I'm trying to figure out where she's going with this. "But I also want a man who loves me enough to respect our commitment."

"And Andrew does?"

"Of course, I wouldn't be with him if he didn't."

Mom pulls her patio chair closer to mine. "Then, I think you should honor your commitment to Andrew and go back to Iowa City right away," she says.

I'm stunned. "But, what about us? We're just getting used to one another, having such fun together." I paused a second. "What about . . ."

"Brad?"

"Well, he's our friend and there are so many things we have planned to do while the weather's still nice," I say.

"That's the problem. I think you and Brad are seeing too much of each other."

"What are you talking about?" I get up and walk away from her, turn my back on her.

"I'm talking about this relationship you have with Brad."

"Friendship, not relationship!" I am adamant.

"You may think friendship, but I promise you Brad is thinking sex."

"My God you are so warped." I say turning around to face her. "Everything's not about sex. Brad's not like that!"

"I think I'm a better judge of that than you are. I've known him quite a bit longer."

"I've known him all my life," I say.

"Sure, when you were in grade school and high school. You've only known him a few months as an adult. Besides, you always told me you'd never get mixed up with a married man like I did."

"You think Brad is a jerk like Edmund?"

"He's married, Megan, doesn't that tell you enough?"

"Mom, this is a friendship, just like Andrew and Lucy. You were wrong about that and you're wrong about this."

"You and Brad are not like Andrew and Lucy!"

I am beginning to chill, even though the night air is warm. "What do you mean?"

"Didn't you tell me that Andrew and Lucy spend most of their time doing things together that you did with them? Missing you together?"

"Yes, that's what Lucy said, and I trust them."

"How much do you miss Andrew when you and Brad are out on the Katy Trail, riding a tandem bike? Or at the winery watching a sunset together? Does he mention Marian anymore at all? Has he told you that she's gone to Ohio to decide whether or not she's going to divorce him?"

"She's in Ohio visiting her folks for the summer."

"That's true. But she's also there to get over the pain of Brad having one too many affairs."

"How do you know all this?"

"Marian told me. And I've known Brad a long time. He's not your friend," she says. "Not if you mean everything you've said about being faithful. I promise you one night when I'm not here and you are walking in the garden, he will make his move."

"I would put him in his place." I had already put him in his place several times when he had too much to drink, or I thought he was going beyond flirting.

"You'd try, but Brad would think you were being coy, think you wanted him to force you. He'd push you down in a grassy part of the garden, away from the light, where no one in the neighborhood could see you or hear you. You'd struggle, but his weight and his strength would be too much."

"Mom, stop it. I can't listen to this anymore. You're jealous!" The words came out of my mouth and startled me, not Mom.

"Why would I be jealous if nothing's going on?" she asked.

"I don't know why you're doing this? Telling me lies."

"Have I ever lied to you?"

I hear the sound of my own thoughts. *No, you've never lied to me. But how could you know this? Unless?*

My mother is reading my mind. "Unless it happened to me," she said.

The full shock of her words hit me, and I had to sit down. We were both quiet for a while.

"When?"

"A few years after the divorce. He was helping me with the yard that spring. It was the year I put in this iris garden."

"How could you have let it happen?"

"You're a woman of the nineties, Megan. You should know that women don't let rape happen! Men make it happen!"

"And you still let him in your house? Around your daughter?"

"I never left you alone with him. Never."

"How could you let him around me at all?"

"How would I explain to Marian? To anyone else for that matter? With my reputation, they'd either think I was lying or that I seduced him. No, it was much better to just put it out of my mind and go on."

"You are telling me you were raped, and you could just put it out of your mind and go on! Oh God, Mom. I didn't know."

She nodded, but a great sadness fell over her like a cloak.

"I didn't want you to know, ever. Don't worry though. It doesn't bother me." She was lying to herself again. I could see how thinking about it made her feel.

This woman, my mother, stands up, walks towards her mother's iris beds, and begins talking to me again. "You know, your grandmother was raped when she was a teenager. It was one of those evangelical ministers who used to travel around and have tent meetings."

I walk over to her and put my arm in hers.

"Aunt Boots told me about it," Mother says, stopping by the edge of the irises. "We were talking about the William Kennedy Smith trial. Boots said the girl was asking for it, going back to the Kennedy place with him. 'I can't understand

why women today make such a fuss about being raped,'"
Boots said.

"You've got to be kidding, Mom."

"No, I wish to God I were. I got really mad," Mom says.
"One of the few times Boots and I have fought. Your Great
Aunt Boots never blames the man, always the woman. It was
the way she was raised."

"Was it the way you were raised, Mom?"

"No, but the way I was raised was just as warped, I guess.
Your grandma lied about things, pretended everything was
wonderful when it wasn't, like when my dad was running
around."

Mom is turning away from the garden now, walking slowly toward the house, the home where she taught me that I was
worthy of respect and that I should expect it from everyone,
especially men.

I squeeze her hand. "You want to come upstairs with me
and help me pack. I think I'll go home to Iowa City tomorrow. If I saw Brad now, I might kill him."

"Don't be silly. For all he knows I've forgiven and forgotten."

"Will you be able to get along here by yourself? "

"Yes. Boots is better. I can come home every weekend,"
Mom says. "Don't you think you ought to call Andrew first?
He may be enjoying the bachelor life so much that he won't
want you to come home."

"Yeah, Mom, like he's going to turn away the best woman
he'll ever find."

She smiles and I realize that despite her insecurities she has
instilled the self-confidence I have.

"Are you going to bed?" I say.

"No, hon. I think I'll just sit outside a bit longer and watch the night some more. The summers go by so quickly now."

I will remember her there, on the patio, by the iris gardens.

About the Author

Marilyn Hope Lake, Ph.D. writes short fiction, poetry, plays, and children's picture books. Lake has won many awards for her writing, including First Place in the 2011 Doris Mueller Poetry and Prose Contest for a children's story. Dr. Lake has been published in *Rock Springs Review, STIR, Well-Versed: Literary Works, the Gasconade Review, the Mizzou Alumni Magazine,* and *105 Meadowlark Reader.* Born in a Mississippi River town, Lake's love of the river shines through her stories. She resides near family in Missouri with her canine companion, Hugo.

Acknowledgments

Versions of the following stories were first published in the following journals:

"Solitaire," *STIR*. University of MO–Columbia Journalism School creative magazine. December 1990. Columbia MO.

"Leaving," *Rock Springs Review*. Vol. 1:3, Spring 1997. RSR Publishing. Boonville MO.

"Lies and Consequences," *Rock Springs Review*. Vol. 2, Spring 1999. RSR Publishing. Boonville MO.

"A Special Family Sunday," *Well-Versed: Literary Works 2012*. Missouri Writers Guild: Columbia Chapter, Columbia MO. (Abridged version of "A Special Family Sunday.")

Awards:

"Boots–The Black Sheep," First Place in the "2011 Dr. Doris Mueller Poetry and Prose Contests" for a story for children. University of Missouri-St. Louis. St. Louis MO. (An abridged version of "The Black Sheep.")

"Solitaire," Second Place Short Story Contest, Southeast Missouri Writers Guild, 2014.

Books are a way to explore, connect, and discover. Reading gives us the gift of living lives and gaining experiences beyond our own. Publishing books is our way of saying—

We love these words,
we want to play a role in preserving them,
and we want to help share them with the world.

...celebrating one woman's life amid the inevitable challenges and joys of long-ago rural living.

—Jean-Ellen Kegler, Center for Joyful Living

Jerilynn Jones Henrikson

...a journey not only to a point on a map but to a whole and liberated self...

2021 Thorpe Menn Award

...upends the fairy stories that confine us, remakes old tropes to break through fear...

I never underestimate
the power of a single puzzle
piece. It fits within a whole,
like each moment of my
unfolding life story.
—Denise Low

Fresh and inviting—
a memoir in lean vignettes...

Kansas Notable Author
Cheryl Unruh

Gravedigger's
Daughter

Ann of Sunflower Lane
Julie A. Sellers

*In a couple of months,
Ann Alwyn's dad will get a
real job, and this whole neglect
thing will be cleared up.*

*She's only at Sunflower Lane
for the summer, she's certain.*